Critical acclaim for
Taste the Bright Lights

'This is the most terrifying book I've ever read...It's scary [illegible] eading. Exem[illegible] g and could[illegible] ct, I'm still ha[illegible]

'...one [illegible] really, seriou[illegible] d it all felt v[illegible] - this book deserves to be much better known.'

'A powerful book that should be on all parents' buying list. Canning's writing is that rare thing in the world of books: original and totally honest. My teenagers loved this book and have given it five stars.'

'Stunning, gritty, heartbreaking.'

'Breathtaking...I finished it in one swoop and was totally amazed by it. Outstanding. By God it deserves a hearing.'

'This book completely knocked me sideways. Laura Canning's portrayal of the forgotten and misunderstood youth of today is vivid and shocking. It is fresh and original and speaks for the disenchanted voice of a generation much like Catcher in the Rye would have done to the youth of the 50s.'

'Epic Northern Irish novel...this book will become a classic.'

‘...destined for great things, one of those “important” novels that critics sometimes harp on about. All teenagers should read this book. One day I’m sure this book will be handed around the classroom as a lesson in what NOT to do after school. This is grim reality. But with that in mind, I’d recommend it to anyone, teenagers and adults alike.’

‘…both brutally stark and genuinely touching...highly recommended.’

‘…remarkable work - should be a compulsory text on every educational curriculum.’

‘…a powerful, vivid and enjoyable book, very highly recommended for both adults and teenagers. Incidentally, although it is set in Northern Ireland, the experiences of the characters are those of urban adolescents across the “developed” world and will be recognized as clearly in London or New York as in Belfast.’

‘A work of complete honesty and authenticity. Should be on the school syllabus as a warning to children and teachers alike.’

Laura Canning grew up in Craigavon, N. Ireland, where much of *Taste the Bright Lights* is set. She now works as a writer and editor in London, and is currently writing her second novel, a sequel to Taste the Bright Lights. Her published journalism and contact details are available at her website www.lauracanning.net.

Taste the Bright Lights

Laura Canning

Taste the Bright Lights
Laura Canning

Airstrip One Publications

First edition 2008
Second edition 2010
Kindle edition 2013
Third edition 2014
ISBN 978-0-9556855-3-8

Part I
Everyone

1.

I don't know where to start, if I'm trying to tell it. How I ended up here? What happened with my ma? The baby?

Always begin at the beginning, my annoying oul cow of an English teacher used to say. Like you can begin anywhere else. She always used to say as well, *Make sure you have a beginning, a middle and an end*, but it'll be a long time before there's an end to my story. I've got a bit of a beginning and a bit of a middle, but for any more, tough, I don't know it myself.

Stuff it. I'll do what she calls 'the who what why when where', then say how it all happened from there.

Who: me, obviously, and Nicola, and the night it started our other mates Leanne Paddy and Marie was there as well. There was some other people there too but they don't count, they were just there and they had their own wee groups to hang around in. There was some fellas as well but I'll get to them later.

So, me. I'm called Lisa O'Neill and I'm fourteen and I live with my ma who's called Carol and my stepda who's called Paul. I have two wee brothers who're twins and they're called Anthony and Ryan. Well, they're not my real brothers cos Paul's their da, but if I say they're my half brothers Paul goes mental. I'd be happy if they weren't even my quarter brothers cos they're wee gits as far as I'm concerned. I hate Paul as well, but my ma says I only don't get on with him because I'm a grumpy bad tempered bitch. She's a charmer, my ma.

Anyway, that's me. Nicola's fourteen as well and she's my best mate. We've been best mates since we were in primary school and we stick up for each other no matter what.

Leanne's thirteen and she lives next door to Nicola. She's in the same class as Paddy who's a girl and is Paddy short for Patricia. Marie's her wee sister and she's twelve. We slag her off a lot cos she says dicky things sometimes. It's Paddy who usually starts the slagging but sometimes she sticks up for her if she's feeling sisterly.

The What is what we were doing, and that's sitting under a bridge with about ten other people, drinking. There's loads of bridges where we live cos there's a river runs right through all the estates down to the lakes. The river's brown and small and smells of shit.

That's the what. Why is cos it's a laugh, obviously, and When is it's half eight on a Saturday night. We'd been out since after our teas cos we all told our mas we were going to the under 18s club night at the community centre and we were getting ready at Nicola's house. That gives us longer to get drunk and sober up in time to get home for half eleven when the club's over. I have to be in at ten, but. Paul'd rather see me raped and murdered doing what he thinks is walking home from the club on my own than let me stay out the same time as my mates. I'm always OK but cos Nicola and the rest of them walk me home cos of course we're not at the club at all.

And the Where is where we live, a grim wee town, well not even a town, a hole, stuck in the middle of nowhere and called Craigavon. It's not too bad growing up there cos there's loads of fields and stuff you can play cops and robbers in, but after you're about ten it's shit. There's nothing to do except sit in doorsteps and hang around, as my ma puts it, cheapening ourselves on street corners (my ma's one to talk, you should see the state of her. She has a leopardskin dress and she wears it with matching shoes). There's a youth club but it's on Saturday nights and it finishes at nine and who's going to go to a youth club and play table tennis instead of going out getting blocked with their mates?

The bit of Craigavon we live in has our school in the middle of it and another big school just across the field from it. There's the reccy which is the leisure centre, and the library, and loads of shit wee pubs the neighbours drink in. There's a shopping centre which is always being advertised on TV by posh shiny people who wouldn't be seen dead in the place, and there's a big lake which is a good place to drink a carryout at. The lake's always full of cider bottles and beer tins.

I don't know how anyone likes Craigavon, how anyone actually decides to live here. We can't help it cos we're forced to. My ma says she likes it and that it's nice and quiet but that's only cos she's thirty five and dead from the neck up. I don't think Paul likes it too much really, but he's the type would only be happy in a big mansion with a sports car and a swimming pool and a troupe of blonde Page 3 girls hanging round his neck. And even then he'd probably moan that their boobs were plastic.

There was loads of things that made what happened happen, but mostly it was cos of Paul and my ma. I hate them. People think you're all stroppy when you're fourteen, you stay out late and take loads of drugs and make your ma and da all worried. They don't know what it's like, living with people who hate you and thump you, but who control your life anyway. If you say anything you get hit and if you run away the peelers always believe them and take you back home. I hadn't a clue a few months ago.

I went to live with my ma when I was five. Before that I was living with my granny but she died so my ma had to take me back. I don't remember living anywhere else before that. I don't really remember much about living with my granny either. The house was dark and brown and I didn't like the food she gave me and she always smacked me and my room was small and cold. I don't remember my ma ever coming to see me so I cried when she came to take me cos I didn't know who she was. I don't think my granny ever told me anything about her and I don't remember asking. I was a quiet wee kid. I just got on with things.

But one day I came home from school and there was a lot of people at the front door, and when they saw me they went all quiet so I thought I'd done something. Some old lady who lived next door took me inside and said, Your granny's away to heaven. I said Why, and she said, God wanted her. What about my tea, I said, my granny always makes me my tea. I'll make you your tea, she said, but I still didn't catch on, I still thought my granny was coming back.

I stayed with the old lady next door for a few days, and I think now they were going to put me into care cos I had to talk to a woman who must've been a social worker. Everything I told her she wrote down and there were loads of times she was talking to the neighbour and I wasn't allowed in. But then my ma came back and I had to go and live with her.

I didn't know my ma when I saw her, she didn't look like a ma at all. She came into the neighbour's house and hugged me a bit and I pulled away. But the neighbour came downstairs with my stuff and said I was going to live with my ma now. I didn't mind I suppose. I'd thought my ma was in heaven with my granny but if everyone said this woman was my ma then she must be, and it was better than living with the neighbour. So me and my ma got on a bus and came to her house. It was dark and cold like my granny's.

I didn't like living with my ma, but I hadn't really liked living with my granny either, and when you're only a tiny kid you just have to put up with things. I thought that's just how things were. But it wasn't fair, any of it. My ma hit me far more than my granny had and it was hardly ever for anything that was my fault. I'd get up in the morning and she'd hit me cos her alarm hadn't gone off so we'd slept in. I'd spill a dribble of milk from my cereal on the table and she'd hit me. She was always in a bad mood and always shouting at me, and the house was always dark and cold. When I think of myself at that age I always see myself crying.

But the next year Paul came to live with us and that was even worse. My ma just ignored me and left everything up to him as soon as he was living with us, especially after she had the two devil children later that year. He got picking if I got to do things, and he always said no and always hit me if I said why. He didn't hit me the way my ma did either. My ma could really belt, she would hammer you and have you sniffling tears and snot in the corner, but Paul punched, he beat you up. Every weekend, every single one, there would be a time where I'd be lying on my bed cos he'd hit me, lying there not even crying cos it was too sore. And it was the unfairness of it that got to me, even at six and seven and eight, when I caught on from school that my ma was different from the other ones. I didn't have to do anything to get hit. I wasn't a bad kid. I would see other mums and dads with their kids, laughing and playing with them, and I'd feel so sad that I wanted to die from it.

I ran away the first time when I was about nine. Paul was even worse cos the devil twins were about three then and they tortured the lot of us so Paul was even more grumpy and thumpy than normal. I thought that if I ran away then my ma would realise how much I hated Paul and she'd kick him out. I should've knew better by that age but I can be pretty thick sometimes.

Anyway, I ran away. I had it all worked out and planned like a military operation. I stashed food for a couple of weeks, nicking the odd tin from the kitchen cupboard and putting it in my wardrobe. I lifted a box of matches one day from the living room. I knew as well I should nick money from Paul's jeans or from my ma's purse but I didn't dare.

Once I'd made up my mind I was going I was really impatient, and it was hard to wait til I thought I had enough stuff, but I made myself. Then one Saturday I got up really early, and I got my bag with the food and the matches and my school jumper in it. And I just left. There was a bit just down the road where I wanted to go back, but when I looked back at the house the light had gone on and I knew if I went back my ma would hit me for being out so early. So I just went on.

The peelers brought me back that night. I didn't know outside our estate that well and I wandered miles and got lost. I didn't get lost enough but, I should've gone miles away into the countryside, burrowed my way in and found somewhere to hide. But I stuck too close to one of the main roads so it was easy enough to find me when they were driving along. They caught me and brought me back home and Paul near killed me. I was trying not to let the peelers know who I was cos I thought if they didn't know my name they couldn't take me back home. But my ma had phoned up and said I was missing, so they knew who I was. I don't know why my ma bothered reporting me missing cos she didn't seem all that glad to have me back. She probably only did it cos she didn't want anyone asking why she hadn't. Anyway, I had to stay in bed all day on Sunday cos I was too sore and bruised to get up. At school on Monday I couldn't do PE and I had to let on I'd fell down the stairs cos I was too scundered to say my ma's boyfriend had beat me up.

The next time I was twelve and I thought that's it, I'm going to do it proper so I don't have to come back ever. So I nuck twenty quid from Paul's jeans one Saturday night when him and my ma were lying asleep. I waited til a Saturday night cos I knew they'd come back pissed and there'd be less chance of them waking up. But it was still one the scariest things I've ever done. Creeping into their room which smelt of sweat and beer, picking up his jeans and holding the belt in my fist so the buckle wouldn't jangle and wake them up, going through the pockets fast, fast, knowing if he woke up and caught me he'd put me in hospital. But I found a twenty pound note and that did me, I didn't bother about the change I could hear in the other pocket. I went back to my room and waited til dawn and then I was away again.

I almost made it down south on the Dublin train but they caught me at Newry and brought me back home in a peeler car. After the peelers were away Paul threw me across the kitchen. I mean really threw me, he picked me up and hurled me into the cupboards. When I woke up I was lying heaped on my bed and I woke up more angry than I've ever felt in my whole life. I was raging at Paul for doing it and at my ma for watching and telling him to go on, but I was raging at the peelers as well. You'd think if someone runs away from home more than once that the peelers'd twig something's wrong, or at least ask if it was. But they just dumped me at home and they must've known from Paul's face I was going to get a hammering. They just didn't care. They were probably glad because they'd had to look for me.

Anyway, I was raging when I woke up and I didn't care what happened to me then and I still don't. I just have to get the next couple of years in so I can leave this hole of a place and live on my own.

2.

At half eight we were well on the way to getting drunk, specially me cos I was drinking a bit faster than everyone else cos like I say I had to be in ages earlier cos of Paul. I was leaning against the wall of the bridge thinking about this, and scowling a bit, and looking into the black water of the river when I saw a shadow on it. Then it moved, and I heard something, then there was a peeler sliding down the embankment. I turned round to hiss —Peelers! and there was two more coming under the bridge from the other side.

We all jumped then froze, except for Nicola who slid her Smirnoff Ice bottle quietly up her sleeve. That's always a good move but it was a bit harder for me cos I was on a two litre cider barrack buster, so I just slid gently out of my coat and dropped that over the bottle and hoped the peelers wouldn't notice.

They started asking everyone's stats and we all got our false names and dates of birth ready so they might leave us alone if they thought we were eighteen. But there was this tube in our year, Gonzo Foster, and he was blocked and acting all Rebel Without a Clue, wobbling about and squinting at them from under his baseball cap. —What do yis need to know *my* name for? he was saying, like he thought he was famous or something. I thought, Shut up you dick, before you get us all lifted. One of the peelers was starting to swell up and go purple, and I was getting scared, cos if you annoy them then they'll lift you, and if I was taken home in a peeler car I might as well sign my suicide note then and there. But one of Gonzo's mates kicked him on the leg and told him to bloody wise up, and Gonzo gave his stats to the peelers OK in the end.

When they'd took everyone's stats they made us give them all the booze that was lying around, and then the gits poured it into the river. Then they said, all menacing, —Don't let us catch yis round here again! Then they were away.

We waited til we knew they definitely were away and not being sneaky, then we started the salvage. I was a happy wee bunny cos they hadn't seen my cider, and Nicola still had her Smirnoff Ice up her sleeve. Leanne had lost the Bacardi Breezer the peelers had seen her drinking but she still had one up a sleeve and another one in her coat. Paddy had stuck her vodka in the waistband of her jeans, and Marie had lost her beer but she was already half cut, same as Gonzo who'd lost his. So it was mostly OK.

But time to move on we thought, we've all heard of peelers coming back five minutes later to check if you've really gone, it's like they don't have anything better to do. We headed to the abandoned estate instead, me and Nicola walking a bit behind everyone. Then when we got there Nicola ses to me,

—Here, Gonzo was really cool there with that peeler wasn't he?

She said it all casual but me not fooled. We never giggle and swoon about fellas, none of us does, but if someone ses a fella's name and it's not in the same sentence as He's a dick – then it usually means something.

—Gonzo Foster! I said. —Are you mad!

—No but, she ses, he was really cool—

—Gonzo Foster! I said. —You fancy Gonzo Foster!

—No I don't! she ses.

I grabbed my throat and let on to swoon.

—Oh Gonzo, I said, —Oh you're so cool with the peelers Gonzo, oh press me to your manly rebellious chest Gonzo—

Nicola thumped me and said I was talking shite, but then she went over to talk to him, so I knew what way her eggs were working. I went over to Leanne and Marie cos I'd seen them light up a smoke.

—After you—

Marie passed me the smoke and her and Leanne went round the bushes to have a piss.

I thought later on that I was a jinx, cos I was the first one to see them again – when I flicked the butt away I saw two peelers melting out of the side of one of the sheds. Shit, I thought, and I looked round to see if I could get away, but it was the same as last time cos of course there was another one coming at us from the other side. They must learn Ambushing at peeler school.

This was shit indeed, cos we all know it's only down to peelers' moods whether you get lifted or not, and we'd already been lucky tonight. I got my face straight and my eyes focused ready to do my Honeshtly offisher I'm as shober as a judge. I had a bit of time anyway cos the two of them by the sheds had found Paddy and Mark in one of them. (Paddy looked well scundered getting scooped with Mark, she always said she wouldn't touch him with a ten foot pole attached to another ten foot pole, so that vodka must work well all right.)

I wondered could I sneaky over to Nicola and Gonzo for a bit of moral support. I eyeballed them. They weren't too far. I started sneakying.

I was nearly there when I heard, —And where do you think *you're* going!

I pulled up like I'd been shot. One of the peelers was tearing up to me.

—I *said*, he shouts, where do you think *you're* going? Did I say *any* of yis could go *anywhere*?

I thought Bloody hell peeler who rattled your cage, it's not CSI here. But then I made my mistake cos I looked over at Nicola. She was near wetting herself laughing, her face was all purple and she had tears coming out of her eyes. When she saw me looking at her she started doing a silent mickeytake of the peeler shouting and of me stood there froze.

Oh god dontlaughdontlaugh, I thought, but a big snort came out of me anyway, and then I heard Nicola giggling.

—Do you think this is *funny*! the peeler ses, eyeballing me like I'd murdered someone. It was a pretty stupid question I thought cos of course I thought it was funny, I was hiccuping and laughing and my eyes were watering. I could hear Nicola snorting with trying not to laugh.

But I caught myself on and wheezed, —No—

I tried to look all sorry and humble as well. I even hung my head for a second before I thought he might think I was taking the piss.

My pathetic looking coupon was too much for Nicola. She let out a huge whoop of laugh, and that was me set off as well.

—***RIGHT***! the peeler shouts, obviously about to get Very Angry Indeed. But then Gonzo jumped forward and shouted Leave them alone, you fat git!

And that was it, the three of us lifted.

3.

The giggles went away pretty bloody quick, you better believe it. It was funny til the door slammed on the copcar, then it wasn't funny so quick you'd've thought my laugh had been killed by the slam. Paul was going to kill me Paul was going to kill me—

Nicola had stopped laughing as well. She was staring out the window with a tragic expression on her coupon, like someone looking out to sea in memory of her dead husband. And me—

I was dead I was dead I was dead.

If the door hadn't of been locked I might've tried to jump out and take my chances with my face being scraped off on the road, but even though peelers are pretty thick they're not that dim. So I sat there while they dropped Gonzo off at his house and we watched him getting dragged in by his ma. But it was worse watching Nicola. Her ma looked all horrified and shocked, and then she looked over to the car at me and made me feel like gurning for what they call letting her down. I really like Nicola's ma, and now she thought I was a cow.

Still, but. Nothing compared to how I felt when the copcar pulled up outside my house. It's probably a mixture of the drink and the fear, but I don't remember getting out of the car, don't remember nothing til Paul opened the door.

—Is this your daughter? the peeler ses to him, pushing me forward a bit (police brutality).

Paul looked at me, all serious so the peeler can think what a good da he is.

—She's the wife's, he ses.

(Charmed, I was.)

The peeler goes,

—Well, we've come across her and her pals

(pals!)

having a drink tonight, and I don't think she's eighteen, is she?

—No, she is not indeed, Paul ses. He let on to give me a dirty look. I say let on cos it was mild for him, he was just putting it on in front of the peeler.

Anyway, I don't remember what else they said, just tutting and young people nowadays and I'll deal with her now officer sort of stuff. The peeler waited til I was inside the house and the door had closed behind me before he went away, so there was no escape.

I don't remember too much either about what happened next, I only have flashbacks. It's always the same anyway. I just remember him shouting at me I was a drunken slut, and I remember laughing at all his empty beer bottles sitting beside the couch. I remember him hitting me. I remember trying to hit him back, and I remember him opening the door and me hitting the wall when he threw me into the hall by my hair and told me to get up to bed now you fat useless slag.

4.

I had a tongue like a budgie cage the next day. People say you don't really get hangovers when you're young, they get worse the older you get, so if that's the case I'd better stop drinking when I'm about eighteen. My head wasn't too sore but my stomach was killing me and I was so thirsty I'd've drank milk straight from the cow. I lay in bed dying for a drink of something, but I didn't want to go downstairs in case my ma or Paul were up. But at some point my ma burst into my room anyway, screaming at me how dare I talk to Paul like that and I was an ungrateful lying wee bitch, and I was grounded for two months, but I could stay in my room the whole time cos no-one in the house wanted to look at me. (She hit me round the head the whole time she was screaming all this, it was the only part of me out of the duvet.)

It was fine by me anyway. Like I wanted to look at them either.

5.

Thank god for school on Monday. Paul and my ma still weren't talking to me, like I was meant to care. But I was dying to get out of the house, and I wanted to see what had happened to Nicola. Her ma and da were all right, but she'd probably still have got killed for bringing the peelers to her door. Parents hate that, but only because it makes them look bad. It's why the kid gets hammered for it, for making the neighbours' curtains twitch. Even Nicola's ma and da might have went mental about it.

Nicola normally called for me but she didn't that morning cos she was scared my ma would shout at her. She waited for me at the end of the road instead. As soon as we saw each other we started laughing. I felt all right.

—Did your ma and da kill you? I said to Nicola. It mustn't've been too bad, cos she looked like she was in a brilliant mood.

—Ach, a wee bit just, she said. —I have to be in at nine every night this week—

See?

—What happened you? she said.

—Nothing, I said. —Grounded. No big deal.

It just shows how crap it is at home when you actually feel better going into school. We got a big YEEOOOWWW! in form class when we walked in, cos everyone'd heard about us getting lifted and we were famous. Kelly Rice, well, Colabottlehead we call her cos her hair's bleached blonde with about six inches of dark roots, anyway, she was sitting on her desk looking like someone had waved a shitty stick under her big nose. She tried to be snattery about it, giving us a dirty look from under all her gel and going, —Hear you got *lifted* the other night, by the *peelers*—

but Nicola just ses to her, —Who else do you think would be lifting us, you stupid bitch—

and Kelly shut her gob pretty fast. She was just jealous anyway. She was really pissed off cos everyone kept asking us what happened and were we scared. They were all wimps, thinking getting lifted was scary. Tony Devlin asked me about the big bruise on my leg and I was dying to say it was the peelers wot done it and I was going to put in a claim, but in the end I just said I didn't know.

It was great being famous. OK, so people were talking to Nicola more, especially the fellas, but it was great anyway. It didn't last though, course it didn't. We had biology first class, and we were on the Reproduction chapter this week, and Conor McVeigh was running around telling everyone we'd have to put condoms on bananas.

Nicola went white.

—Do we? she said to me, all quiet so no-one could hear her.

—I don't know—

I was shitting it a bit now. OK, so I didn't want to look like I knew how to use a condom, cos that would make me a ***SLUT***, but I didn't want to look stupid either. And if I couldn't put it on all the fellas would say Sure what do you expect, she'll never get the chance to touch one of them, who'd go near *her.*

We should've knew Conor McVeigh was taking the piss. Fitzy just waffled on about plants and stamens and seed scattering (Conor started doing hand movements under the table), but there was nothing about people or condoms or anything scundering at all. There was a Human Reproduction bit next in our textbook, but Fitzy just ses, —For your homework you have to read that and answer the questions at the end—

and that was our reproduction class.

But anyway, forget all that. That day was Nicola acting weird. She's pretty confident usually, a lot more than me, so I wouldn't've thought she would've minded even if we had of had to put a condom on a banana. But she was scundered even thinking about it. And then she went all funny in the yard at break time when we were having our smoke. She just took a beamer out of nowhere. I'd only said Did you do your French homework, and I couldn't see what was so scundering about that, I already knew she fancied Antoine the French student teacher.

But then I looked round to the other side of the yard, and there was that dick Gonzo again. He was having a smoke with Conor McVeigh and Tony Devlin, and he was still acting the dick, reeling around and waving his arms about and talking shite. I couldn't hear him but I knew he was.

Then they all looked over at us.

Course I'd like to think they were saying, —Here, isn't that Lisa O'Neill one lovely? but I didn't come down the river in a bubble, so I ses to Nicola, —Maybe Gonzo fancies you.

—Aye right, Nicola ses, but her face was still burning, so I thought it must be her fancying him to make her take the reddener, not that I could see why. The fellas had stopped looking over at us but now they were laughing, and Gonzo was still flailing his arms about like a demented bloody penguin. He really annoyed me. He annoyed me as well cos he was ugly, with his big hooky nose and wee weasly eyes, but girls still go out with him, and I'm ugly as well and none of the fellas'll come near me. Even if a girl's only a wee bit ugly a fella won't go out with her, and him and his mates call her a dog. But a fella can be really ugly and girls will still go out with him. It's not fair.

I never get going out with anyone, and I'd get laughed at if I asked. I know people sometimes say they're ugly and they're not, they have that body morph thing or they're just fishing for compliments, but I really am. (And that's why I'd never say it to anyone.) But people have called me it. One fella used to follow me home when I was in second year, saying every day I was the ugliest girl he'd ever seen. He used to say it real loud as well, so everyone heard him. Every day for three weeks til he got sick of it, for the whole fifteen minutes home, with half the school following him and laughing and going She is isn't she. And my ma never buys me any new clothes so I've only got one pair of jeans and a couple of tops she doesn't want. The tops are baggy to hide my bum cos the jeans are too small, and people call me fat as well.

And there's that dick Gonzo, uglier than me I think on the scale, and he can go out with anyone and no-one would ever think of calling him ugly. Fellas sicken me sometimes.

6.

By Tuesday night I was climbing the walls. When I came home from school I had to go straight up to my room and stay there all night. I do that normally anyway, cos anything's better than looking at Paul's face, but now I couldn't even go out after my dinner for a smoke. And Anthony and Ryan were near getting threw out the window cos they kept coming into my room to torture me, cos they knew I couldn't do anything cos then Paul would kill me more.

School was getting shit now as well, cos Nicola was no company cos she was still acting weird. She kept shouting Piss off to Tony Devlin and Conor McVeigh when they were whispering and sniggering and nudging each other. But I couldn't see why, cos they do that all the time anyway, they think they're great. Nicola said she knew it was about her. But she didn't say why.

Anyway, we went in on the Wednesday morning, but as soon as we got in through the door Tony and Conor started laughing again. They were looking at Nicola this time though right enough. Then Conor looked right at Nicola, and then he said,

—But I don't know what to *doooo*!

and him and Tony started laughing.

I don't know what it meant, but Nicola went mad. She stormed over to their desk in about two seconds flat, and she lifted her arm up and she whacked Conor round the face. It was so hard he near fell over. And his face, big shocked amazed eyes. It made me smile for weeks after.

Everyone else in the class sat up, they were loving this and they were waiting to see what Conor would do. He probably didn't know himself at first cos the birds were still flying round his head singing. Nicola was still stood in front of him giving him the death stare. Then he copped on everyone was looking at him and waiting to see what he'd do, so he said, —Bitch! at Nicola, and he tried to launch himself over the desk to hit her. But Nicola must've thumped him real good, cos he misjudged the distance and then he got his feet tangled up, and he hit the desk face first. Oh it was beautiful.

—C'mon, Nicola said to me, —do you want to mitch—

—Yeah, I said, and we swept out of the classroom like I was cool.

7.

We'd go nicking up at the shopping centre we thought. This is what I mean about how things just spiralled after Saturday, cos we got caught. Not caught mitching by a teacher which would've been bad enough, but caught nicking by a shop. Peelerss, mas and das called, the lot.

It was the first time caught for me or Nicola, we're normally good at nicking. But she was still in that weird mood and maybe she wasn't careful enough. I don't know. I was keeping the eye out for her and she looked like she was doing everything all right. But we got caught.

We went into Superdrug first, cos we just wanted to nick something, anything, for the laugh, and wee smelly things are the easiest. But there was a snattery shop assistant who kept eyeballing us over the shelves, so we thought we should leave it. I'd been wanting to nick some foundation as well. I know makeup's not going to work like plastic surgery and suddenly make me a supermodel, but it must do something or else people wouldn't wear it. No chance though with Gorilla Features leering at us from over the shampoo.

So we went into JJB Sports cos Nicola said she wanted to rob a Man United shirt. —Who's that for, I said, and she said, —Chris. But she looked a bit guilty when she said it. Chris is her brother and he lives in England, he's class. I didn't think he was coming home, she hadn't said. Anyway, we went down to the back of the shop where the football tops were, and I had a nosy about for the shop assistants. There was a girl at the till stabbing a pricing gun into pairs of shorts like they'd personally offended her, and a fella beside her with big sideburns thinking he was god's gift.

I kept lookout and Nicola pulled the security tag off the top and stuffed it up her jumper. When I turned round to check if she'd finished I near fainted, cos she looked pregnant and it was weird, seeing her like that when I didn't expect it. But then she flattened the top against her stomach so she just looked fat, and we went towards the exit.

Going out of a shop's always the worst bit, cos you never know if they haven't seen you or they're just letting on they haven't, til you're actually out and have actually nuck. Your heart thumps and you wait for the hand on your shoulder,

and this time it came.

The rush of shock I got when I knew we'd been scooped was like being shoved into a tank of cold water. All I could think about was Paul. They called the cops and I know I should've been worrying about that, but I couldn't even think about them. I was still sore from Saturday, and this was far worse.

So, the peelers came in, and we got took home again. We didn't know yet if we had to go to court cos the girl in the shop said it was up to the manager whether to press charges. But stuff court, I thought, I was only worried about Paul and my ma.

My ma was the only one in when the peelers knocked on the door, and when she got me on her own she screamed at me like a banshee. She thumped me til she got too tired to do it any more, and she shouted all the time about Just! You! Wait! Just! You! Wait! Til He Gets Home! But of course that was nothing compared to what happened when he did get home. I'm not even going to write about it cos how many times can you say He hit me.

8.

—What're you looking at?

—A slag—

Nicola's face went red, just like that, in about a second.

—WHAT – DID – YOU – CALL – ME?

Kelly wasn't bothered.

—A slag—

We were in form class waiting for our form teacher Hornball to turn up. It was the day after me and Nicola were scooped for nicking the Man U shirt, and when we came in everyone turned round to look at us the way they do when they've been talking about you. Kelly Colabottlehead was sitting on her desk in front of Tony Devlin and Conor McVeigh, and she stared at us the most. I thought it was something to do with yesterday, but she was mostly looking at Nicola.

She said to Tony and Conor,

—*Here* she is, *now*—

Nicola glared at her. She said, —What are you looking at—

Kelly said, —A slag, and that was it. By the time she said it again Nicola was over at her desk. She pulled Kelly off it by the hair. Kelly bounced to the ground (flashing her skiddy knickers ha ha), but Tony and Conor dived in and pulled Nicola off and picked Kelly up. I pushed forward as well, cos jumping in isn't allowed.

Nicola and Kelly stood glaring at each other, out of breath. They looked like a couple of cats. Kelly pounced first.

—You *are* a slag, she said, —we all know you shagged Gonzo Foster at the weekend—

There was a big dramatic gasp from everyone, I near expected the Eastenders doof-doof to start up.

Nicola shouted, No I didn't!

Tony broke the rules again.

—You did, he said, cos he told me—

—Then he's talking through his hole, I said. I jumped in cos Tony had and we needed two against two, and cos I knew it was all a load of shit. None of us have ever done it with anyone. We'd know.

Then Conor said what he'd said on Monday. And now that I thought about it I'd heard a few times this week as well. He put on a high-pitched voice and went, —But I don't know what to doooo!

And Nicola just screamed, —Shut up!

I turned round to look at her, to see how upset she was, cos if she cried, cried in front of all these bitches, she'd never live it down. And I was going to back her up no matter what, cos she was my best mate and we always back each other up.

And I saw from her face that it was true.

I didn't let on. I'd like to say it was only cos of loyalty to her. But it was really cos I'd already said Gonzo was talking through his hole, and cos if Kelly Rice said black I'd say white just to annoy her. I didn't feel loyal towards Nicola at all right then. I was raging at her.

Nicola had screamed real loud and for a second no-one said anything. It was better than a row in the Queen Vic, this. Nicola's scream floated off the walls. Then Kelly Colabottlehead stuck her face in Nicola's and said, —You know rightly you did. He's *told* us, you slag!

Nicola headbutted her.

Kelly was asking for it anyway, sticking her face in Nicola's range like that. She was lucky cos she saw Nicola's dome coming at her in time to jump back, so she only got watery eyes instead of a bloody nose.

—There's no need to *cry* about it, Kelly, Nicola said, even though she knew fine well Kelly's eyes were watering cos she'd just been clamped in the nose.

Kelly was ripping, she near had steam coming out of her ears. But Nicola turned her back on her and then she said to me, —Are you coming out for a smoke?

Yeah I bloody am, I thought, cos I wanted to know why my best friend hadn't told me about the most important thing you could tell your best friend about. We slammed out.

By the time we got round the side of the block I could see Nicola was scundered, she knew I knew. But I didn't care, I was raging. I couldn't believe she hadn't told me, I couldn't believe it. And I couldn't believe she'd done it in the first place. I know that makes me sound like an old granny but I don't mean it like that. I mean the way you can't do anything like that round here, if you're a girl anyway, without the fella spreading it about to everyone and then everyone calling you a ***SLUT***. We all know who the girl is in year nine who shagged someone at the year eleven party. We know who let someone grope her tits under the bridge on a carryout Saturday. And we know how they're called a ***SLUT*** for doing it. You just can't do anything like that round here, not if you're a girl, not unless it's in deadly secret with a deaf and dumb Australian bloke who's flying back home straight after. I'm dying to know what it's all about but I've got my imaginary chastity belt on til I'm older and no-one can slag me off for it. Or til I move away and no-one knows me.

I don't let on to anyone I think about stuff like this, cos thinking about it would still be being a ***SLUT***. And cos they'd just say, —Sure who'd go with that ugly bitch anyway—

Nicola lit our smoke and we stood there for a bit.

—It's not true, she said.

—Aye right!

I could've hit her. I was her best friend.

—Why didn't you tell me?

—It's not true!

—I know it's true, I said, —I can see it in your face—

She didn't deny it quick enough this time, then she didn't deny it at all.

I got even madder. I can't explain it, I was just so angry at her. This was the biggest thing that could happen and she hadn't told me. I would've told her.

—Why didn't you tell me? I shouted at her.

—I don't have to tell you everything!

—Yeah, but you could've told me this!

—I don't have to tell you everything, Lisa! she shouted back.

—I know, I said, but you could've told me this, it's a big deal—

I said it calmly enough but Nicola flipped. She looked straight at me and blew smoke out and said, —Why're you so bothered anyway? Cos you know no fella'll ever go near you —

I should've said —No fella at all is better than that ugly git you shagged, but her saying that had been like when you fall flat on your stomach, like out of a tree when you're a kid, and all the air goes out of you. I knew if I opened my mouth I would start crying. And I didn't want to start an argument on *ugly* anyway, the ice was too thin. Sometimes people say something to you and it's like being smacked around the face, you can't breathe. I just stood there in goldfish mode, moving my mouth but not saying anything, and I watched Nicola as she swung her bag over her shoulder and strode off back into school.

9.

The next week was a nightmare. Swear to god, I think it was the worst week of my life, at least til then. Nicola wasn't speaking to me and I definitely wasn't going to speak to her after her saying that. She didn't come back to school on the Thursday so that wasn't too bad, but the next day, the Friday, she came in and it was terrible cos everyone knew right away we'd fell out. We sit at the same desk so it was really obvious, cos we sat there beside each other not speaking. Or rather I sat there, Nicola went to speak to loads of other people and I couldn't do the same cos it'd look like I was only doing it cos she was (and I can't do that anyway, how do you just go up and just start talking to people without sounding like a dick?). People like Nicola better anyway. They always do.

So I had to go and sit in the bogs at break time cos there's nothing sadder than standing in the yard on your own, cos only the weirdoes do that, the ones who smell and who everyone laughs at. You can't sit and read or something cos that's pathetic. And if you get caught out, like when you get there too early for class after lunch but everyone's already there waiting for the teacher to come and unlock the door, you have to stand by yourself looking like you don't care, looking aloof and interesting. And you have to have the right expression as well. Not letting on to smile cos then everyone'll think you're a looper, standing there smiling to yourself, but not with a big sour bake on you, cos then they'll think you mind. You have to just look like you're looking at something a wee way off, and you have to keep your face all bright and casual. It's harder than you'd think. And it bloody knackers you.

By lunchtime my face hurt and I was sick of it all, so I just left. I couldn't go home, cos my ma was off work today and cos she was still thumping me for nicking the Man U top. For *Nicola* nicking the Man U top. So I went and sat under a bridge.

I didn't even get peace there, cos people from our school kept coming past on their way home to lunch. Any time I saw someone coming I let on to look all busy and concerned, like I was only sitting there cos I had to look in my bag for something. I was sick of this. If it had of been the olden days I'd've run away to sea. I'd be good at that, I'd be one of them girls who lets on to be a fella. It's always crap in films when girls let on to be fellas cos it's so obvious they're not. Your woman in Shakespeare in Love no more looked like a fella just cos she had a wee stick-on tache. But I could look like a fella no bother if I had to. I'd strap my boobs down and run away to sea and swashbuckle about for a bit, and if anyone annoyed me I'd slice their heads off with my sword. Hah. Take that, you dastardly cad—

A couple of girls in the class beside ours walked past and caught me daydreaming. I heard them laughing after they went past. Bitches.

When I went back after lunch Nicola was sat with Julie and Natalie and Anne-Marie, and they were all huddled round Julie and Natalie's desk giggling. When I came in they looked up, and Anne-Marie said something and they all looked at me and laughed. Of course I had to let on I hadn't noticed, or I didn't care anyway, so I just went to my desk and took a book out and pretended to read it and imagined slicing Anne-Marie's head off. How come Nicola can make friends with people and I can't? Probably no-one liked me anyway, probably they only put up with me just cos I was Nicola's mate and everyone liked her no matter what. No-one was even mentioning now about her and Gonzo shagging—

As soon as the bell went for hometime I scarpered. I walked fast down the corridor with my head down, fast away from being so sad and embarrassed and ashamed. But all there was to go was home.

The next week it just got worse. When I got up in the morning I felt sick about going to school. And I felt really really exhausted with having to let on I didn't care, and not show myself up or give anyone ammunition by letting them see how sad and tired and upset I was. I felt jittery all the time and my eyes felt shiny and hot and too small. I broke a cup in the kitchen on Thursday morning cos I just suddenly couldn't hold it any more, so my ma sent me into school already crying.

I would've given anything, my right arm, anything, just to be on my own. Up in a cabin in the mountains, with a log fire and melting snow in a kettle and no-one else around for miles. As soon as I was sixteen and the cops couldn't make me go back home I was packing a bag and leaving, I didn't care where.

Kelly Colabottlehead and her mates were loving it that me and Nicola weren't sticking up for each other any more. First thing on Monday Kelly homed in on me like a vulture who's seen its dinner.

—Why's you and Nicola fell out? she ses, leaning over my desk letting on to be all concerned. Her eyes were bright with fun she was so concerned.

—Just—

—But *why*? she ses.

—Just, I said!

I know I shouldn't even have answered her, or I should've told her where to go, but you can't when you've no mates and everyone's fell out with you. I'd have licked a leper rather than have Kelly Colabottlehead for a mate but I couldn't handle a proper feud with her at the same time I was fighting with Nicola. I wasn't strong enough to deal with her, and she knew it.

—Nicola ses it's because you're a nosy bitch, Kelly ses, sounding all confidential like she didn't know the whole class was listening.

I didn't say anything.

—Are you? Kelly ses.

I didn't say anything.

—*Are* you a nosy bitch?

I said,

—Piss off Kelly, right—

It was stupid cos it was what she wanted. But I couldn't help it.

—Oooooohhhh! she screeched, like Graham Norton being sarky. I wanted to thump her but I wasn't strong enough, so I kept looking down at the homework I was letting on to do.

She got annoyed I wasn't looking at her.

—Here, she said, and she poked me in the arm with her ruler, —don't you be talking to me like that—

I didn't say anything.

—Right? she said, poking me with the ruler.

I didn't say anything.

—*Right*? she said, poking me again.

I just looked hard at my book cos I suddenly felt really really sad, and it was drowning me and I couldn't think of anything else, and I was near gurning. I'd've rather died, I swear, really died right there, than let any of those bitches see me cry. I couldn't blink cos the tears would've dropped, so I stared at my book and dug my nails in my hand and prayed for the tears not to get bigger and fall.

—Are you *deaf*? Kelly ses, poking me again.

That was it, it was either cry or fight back. So I looked up and got ready to tell her where to go. But my eyes were wet and when I blinked in the light of the classroom a tear rolled down my cheek!

I was so totally, quickly, scundered it was like someone'd threw boiling water over me. A big cheer went up. Kelly waved her ruler about like a conductor.

—She's *crying*, everyone! The big yap's *crying*! One two three, *awww*!

I tried to say —No I'm not—

but the words wouldn't come out and I knew if I tried too hard I'd cry properly cos it'd been building up. Everyone looked at me, all I could see was laughing. It was like one of those black and white films where someone's trousers fall down and everyone points and roars at them, and they just stand there looking stupid.

I did the only thing I could now and I took a swipe at Kelly. But she jumped back easily.

—*Oooohh*! she went again.

—She's blind as well! someone shouted.

—Can't see for the tears—

Killing Kelly or at least bashing her head in off the wall was probably the only way I could get out of this now. But then the door opened and Nicola came in.

My stomach jumped and I waited to see what she'd do. Nicola hated Colabottlehead as much as I did, and anyway you stick up for your best mate no matter what. OK, so we'd fell out, but this was more important.

Kelly thought this too, you could tell. She looked at Nicola looking a bit scundered, like a babysitter caught torturing the kid. Then she tried to do salvage.

—Here Nicola, she said, —the nosy bitch's a yap as well—

I waited for Nicola. We might have fell out but she'd be raging about Kelly letting me know Nicola had been talking to her about us.

Nicola came fully into the room. She said,

—Sure I know that already—

Then she gave me a dirty look and she sat down at her new seat beside Anne-Marie.

It was the worst thing I could've done but I couldn't help it. I ran out of the room. I could hear everyone laughing behind me.

10.

So that was Monday. On Tuesday Tony Devlin told me in front of everyone I was a fat dog and the only way anyone would ever go out with me would be if I paid them a million quid (I said back, —Well I wouldn't go out with *you* even *for* a million quid, which I thought was pretty good considering. But everyone just laughed at me anyway). On Wednesday in PE Kelly waited til McGrath wasn't looking then she threw the netball ball right in my face. This was after no-one would pick me for their netball team and I had to stand there like a lemon until McGrath made Nicola's team take me and then everyone moaned. Thursday was Kelly and her cronies sitting talking about me in really loud voices with everyone listening, and me sitting at my desk letting on I couldn't hear them and that I didn't care anyway. I hated Kelly so much I shook when I thought of her, I wanted to kill her.

Then she banged into me on purpose in the yard at break time and I went flying. There was a gasp and a snigger from round me when I hit the ground so I knew I'd flashed my knickers to everyone, and minging old blue ones as well that I'd had for years.

I got up. I was so angry I was seeing spots in front of my eyes. I think it was cos it was near the weekend, so even after school was over I knew I'd still not get peace, I'd have to sit in the house with my ma and Paul and the devil children, and Paul normally thumped me when he was drinking. It was like Monday in form class, when I felt so sad it was like water just rushing over me. Only this time it wasn't sad but anger.

I checked for teachers. There wasn't any, so I stormed over to where Kelly and her cronies were laughing at me. She saw something in my eyes and she stepped back a bit. But then she wanted to save face so she squared up.

—What's *your* problem? she said.

She used that snattery voice she puts on when she's trying to act hard. I didn't care any more. I said, —You, you bitch—

And I launched myself at her.

I could hear shouts and I could feel everyone closing round us to hide the fight from the teachers, but I didn't care now even if I did get caught. I grabbed her hair with both hands and I jerked her head down. I'd never fought so well. I was going to beat her easy, I knew it.

All I could hear now was the blood roaring in my ears. I kept her head down and I twisted her round. I was trying to rip her hair and get her to the ground cos once she fell I was going to kill her. Her hands were on my arms cos she was trying to get free, but then she let one go and fisted it and punched me in the face. I didn't even feel it. I brought my leg up and kicked her in the knee, hard. She wobbled, toppled, fell. Timberrrrrrr.

I was on her fast before she could get up. You've pretty much won the fight when they fall, all you have to do is jump on them and bash them til they say they give up. I held her arms above her head, and I put my knee on her chest, and I just pushed into her til she said, —Stop—

—What? I said. I'd heard her of course, but I wanted to make sure everyone else did.

—Stop, she said, —I give up—

I gave her chest one last, hard, dig, and I got up. I looked round at everyone, but there was just silence. In a film I would've won the crowd over with my skill and nerve, and some people would've come over and pumped my hand and said quietly Good job there mate. Then we would've laughed evilly at Kelly, haw haw haw, and I would've walked off into the sunset with my new friends' arms round me.

Some chance. They all just stood there gawping at me. They were pissed off cos I'd won. I didn't care. I hated all of them. I pushed past them and got my schoolbag and I went back into the school on my own.

11.

And that was Thursday. Colabottlehead was still raging the next day about being scundered in front of everyone but it was an OK day cos at least she left me alone. But then I heard rumours her and her mates were going to jump me after school and give me a kicking, and it got to me, course it did, cos why couldn't everyone just leave me alone? But still, I was better than I was at the start of the week even if I did have a weekend of Paul in front of me.

I was able to avoid her after school, I just mitched off after lunch and went to the library for a bit, and then I went home five minutes before the last bell would go. I wasn't scared of the bitch but I wasn't going to put myself in front of her and three of her cronies either. I was shitting it a bit over the weekend about going into school on Monday but then it didn't matter, cos on Sunday night there was a stone at my window.

I jumped over to it quick before Paul heard it. He hadn't thumped me this weekend yet apart from a wee punch yesterday but he had a hangover today so I was staying well clear.

I looked out and it was Nicola.

I got a shock first cos she was there and then cos of the way she looked. She'd been crying, and her face was papery white, and she looked so miserable you'd've thought she was about to die.

It flashed into my head for a minute, just a second, I should just ignore her cos of what a bitch she'd been to me. But you can't ignore someone crying. It's not right. And I hated not being mates with her, I really missed her. So I opened the window to lean out.

She whispered up at me,

—Can you get out?

I shook my head no.

She looked like she was going to sit down on the ground and wail.

I hated Paul. I was desperate in case she went away again. But there was no way I could get out, our living room's beside the front door so I'd no chance of sneaking out past him.

She knew this usually. But she didn't say anything yet, I think she was trying to get a hold of herself. Then she said,

—I'll call for you tomorrow, OK?

12.

I lay in bed and wondered why she'd came back. Not that I was complaining like, but why now, and as well what had happened to make her cry. Maybe she just missed me. Aye right, my sarky voice said, and I turned over and didn't go to sleep.

13.

I was dying to get to school the next day. I couldn't've cared less about Kelly and her stupid kicking.

Nicola didn't say anything about the crying yet. She called for me and we walked down to the bridge, but we didn't really say much. I was dying to ask her but we were a bit scundered with each other so I didn't.

Leanne and Paddy and Marie were under the bridge waiting for Nicola, and their eyes near popped out when they seen me with her. They'd said they hadn't fell out with me just cos Nicola had, and they'd always said Hiya when they'd seen me. But they'd sounded a bit scundered and guilty when they said it all the same. And none of them called for me the whole time, or came up to me at breaktime, or talked to me at all apart from Hiya. It had bothered me a bit at the time, but in a way I'd sort of thought it was like more proof that people liked Nicola really. And they lived closer to Nicola, they'd hung around with her for years and they knew her longer. I couldn't blame them, not really.

But now they all said Hiya, properly like it was an OK word again, so now I knew things were back to normal. We had a smoke and we started up the path to the school, just like always. I couldn't wait to get into the form room. I couldn't wait to see Kelly's face when I walked in with Nicola.

But Nicola was hanging back, and when I looked round to see where she was she grabbed my arm.

—Do you want to mitch, she ses.

If I got caught mitching again Paul would break my arm. (True fact. He'd told me.) So I couldn't really.

Nicola must've seen it in my face, cos she said,

—Please, Lisa. I have to talk to you—

Now we're going to get to it, I thought. So I said, —Yeah. All right.

It was raining again. We stood under a door at the back of the community centre. I let Nicola wait to tell me whatever it was. We smoked.

She said,

—You know what Conor and Tony were saying—

I waited.

—About me and Gonzo—

I waited.

—It was true, she said.

—I know, I said.

That mustn't be what she was going to tell me. But there was something I was nosy about anyway. I said, —Can I ask you something?

Me and Nicola don't normally talk to each other like this, all important and serious like we're in some TV programme. But there was something coming, I knew it.

—Yeah, Nicola said.

She didn't say What, she said Yeah. I knew cos of that we were OK again, I could ask her things and she'd tell me and we were all right.

And I knew as well, I don't know how, but I knew that she needed me, she'd come back for something else as well and she needed me.

—You know Conor? I said. —You know when he kept saying, *But I don't know what to doooo—*

She looked scundered but I wanted to know. I said, —What did he mean?

I looked at her for the first time since we'd started talking. She was smiling. But it was a smile like she was about to cry.

—I couldn't get the, em, thing on him, she said. —You know, when me and Gonzo were…he got one from his ma and da's room and he said to put it on him and I said But I don't know what to do. I don't know how to put them on—

Me and Nicola, me and nobody, had ever had a conversation like this before and I was going red, but I said it anyway.

—Do not, em, do not just roll it down his, em—

—It rolls back up, Nicola said. She sounded like she was near crying.

—Oh, I said.

And then she said it.

—Lisa, I think I'm pregnant.

14.

This time I never imagined myself ignoring her. Saying to her, Tough shit, and then just flicking my cigarette into the rain and walking away. This was far too big and it was like the last two weeks had never happened.

I wasn't much good to start with though, I couldn't take it in. It'd been enough, too much, to take in Nicola even doing it with Gonzo. And now here she was saying the worst thing ever, the worst nightmare. I thought, all in a second, about Nicola's ma and da going mental. Nicola getting laughed at in school, getting pointed at and whispered about and called a ***SLUT***. The pitying looks from the teachers. Nicola in her school uniform with a big bump in front, trying to sit down. Nicola with a baby. Flabbergasted is a word I read once, and it just fits how I felt when she told me.

I'm proud to say I didn't stand there catching flies all day, but. I asked her how she knew, was she sure.

She wasn't sure, she didn't know. But she was near two weeks late, and she didn't know if it was just cos she was panicking but she thought she was as well. —My ma ses she knew right away with all of us, she ses you just know, she said.

That sounded a bit hmmm to me but who knew. So I said to her, —Well we could do a test, just so you know one way or the other—

But when I mentioned a test she went a bit mental. She said she probably wasn't, and she was probably just panicking. She kept saying it. I asked her every day for the next week had she took her period yet and she always said no. But she still wouldn't do a test. She was probably just panicking she said, it'd only been a couple of weeks and she was never regular anyway. Then she started saying she knew she was going to get it soon, cos she was getting cramps when she ran up the stairs and that always meant it was going to start in a couple of days. Then she said she'd no money for a test anyway, and she couldn't go to her doctors cos he knew her ma and she'd get killed.

I bullied her. I did it on purpose, like she was a wee kid. I told her she had to know, and she probably wasn't but wouldn't it be good to know she wasn't, and if she didn't do a test, and she was, she'd end up like one of them girls having a baby in the school bogs and being in Take a Break for killing it and trying to flush it down the bog.

She agreed in the end, just to shut me up I think. But she'd said it, even if she did say then she'd only do it if I went in and got it, and only if we got it in a chemist where no-one knew us. We had to mitch off again. I still wasn't allowed out, so we couldn't go into town on Saturday. We mitched on the Monday and I just didn't think about what would happen if we got caught.

We planned it, we brought a change of clothes so no-one'd know we were meant to be in school. Nicola brought a tin of beer as well she'd tealeafed from her dad, cos she was shitting herself and even though it wasn't true she'd still need a Stiff Drink after checking.

We'd no money so we had to walk into town, Lurgan cos it was the closest. We went to the chemist's right at the end of town just in case any of our mas' friends were in town shopping and spotted us in the high street. We'd planned what we were going to do and we went in. Nicola went up to the counter and starting asking about stuff for a rash on her foot, and I found the kits and tried to pick what one.

There were loads of them and I didn't know what one was best or maybe they were all the same, I didn't know. But I had to get one, cos it'd took me a week to get Nicola agreed and if I didn't get it now she'd not agree again. I checked in the security mirror, and I hoped there was no-one in the back of the shop watching me, and I grabbed one of the tests and shoved it up my sleeve.

I went back over to Nicola. She knew I'd got it so she said to the oul woman behind the counter she'd maybe she'd come in later to get that cream she'd said about, and thank you and goodnight. I was near fainting going out of the shop but we got out OK.

We looked round for a bog. The ones in the park were shut. There was ones at the other end of town but they needed 20p and we were stony. Nicola said to try a pub, but when we opened the door of The Cellar the barman gave us a suss look and we thought he wouldn't let us come in. So we ended up going back to the park, and Nicola had to go behind the bushes. She said no but I bullied her again.

She came out of the bushes. She handed me the stick.

—I missed some of it, she said. —I couldn't see—

It'd took us a while to know how the test worked but we did know you had to wait a couple of minutes. Nicola said she couldn't look, I'd have to tell her. So I waited, and I looked, and I knew it, it was positive.

15.

Nicola said it was wrong. She knew it. You couldn't pish onto a stick in the middle of some bushes and expect it to be right. The results, she said, were contaminated—

I said Yeah. Maybe it was wrong. But I only said it to calm Nicola down, cos she looked like she was going to flip. I don't believe it I don't believe it, she kept saying, and then she couldn't even stand, she slumped to the grass and sat there like a broken wee china doll.

She looked up at me, looking scared, looking tiny. I gave her the tin of beer and lit her a smoke and told her what she wanted to hear, maybe the test was wrong.

—It's not, she said now, near biting the top of the smoke off and with her teeth chattering against the beer can. —It's not, I know it's not—

—You *don't* know, I said. I felt like her ma, or a social worker. —You did it in the bushes and missed some of it, you said so yourself. You might have got it wrong—

—But I am, she said. —I know I am, I can feel it—

—Could you, could you not go to the doctor? Get him to double check?

—Lisa no way! He'll tell my ma, even if I'm not!

She was right. We couldn't tell anyone, in case she wasn't and there was a big hassle about nothing.

And if she was—

I said, What do you want to do then?

So I nuck another test from another chemist.

That was positive as well.

We near fought about the third one. I didn't want to freak her out but she had to hear it, if two were positive then it must be true. But she started crying, saying to me Please please Lisa, it might not be, just try one more. So we went to another chemist's.

It was too risky getting another one in Lurgan and the ones in Craigavon were too local, so we had to walk all the way into Portadown. My feet were roasting and throbbing by the time we finally got there. I don't think Nicola noticed her feet. We got another test and the toilets were open and didn't eat 20ps so in we went. I waited outside the cubicle. I could hear the paper rustling and then Nicola pissing. I don't pray but I prayed this one was right.

Nicola came out. For the third time she gave the stick to me. I counted then I looked. Positive.

16.

We didn't talk about it yet. We didn't know what to do, and we were in shock as well probably. We just went home. I left Nicola at her house, all pale with huge eyes, and I just said, I'll see you tomorrow, cos I didn't know what else to say and neither did she.

We went into school the next day cos we had to, if we mitched off any more someone was going to twig and my arm was going to break. But we couldn't talk in form class either in case anyone heard us. And then we couldn't talk anyway cos Kelly Colabottlehead started mouthing off.

She'd been doing it all week, cos she was still scundered and pissed off about me winning the fight, and then when she saw me and Nicola were mates again she knew she couldn't just start picking on me to make herself look better. So she mouthed a bit, mostly when Nicola wasn't there and always in front of everyone else, how she was going to give me a kicking, I'd only won the fight cos she wasn't well that day and I'd knew it and that's why I'd fought her. It wasn't fair and she was going to get me back.

I'd just ignored her all week, not even pretending she wasn't getting to me cos she really wasn't. I had a maybe pregnant Nicola to think about and it made Kelly sound about ten the way she was getting on. She wasn't important, and I wouldn't even be telling about her now if it hadn't of been for what happened that day.

Maybe today was more urgent for her cos it was Friday, maybe she'd decided in her tiny empty wee head that it was this week she was going to get me so it had to be today. You'd've thought she'd've knew there was no chance now cos I was friends with Nicola again. But that's Colabottlehead for you, thick as a lump of frozen shite.

Anyway, me and Nicola were just sitting there, not even with our coats off yet, and not saying anything cos we couldn't talk about It and we didn't feel like saying Did you see Hollyoaks last night. But Kelly must've thought we'd fell out again.

I was thinking about It but I could sort of hear her voice in the background, and I was sort of aware it was getting louder and louder, like the buzz from a fly to a bluebottle. Then I looked up and there she was.

Like I say, she should've knew, but Kelly's always lived in airhead city. She started in straight away.

—What's wrong with you today, O'Neill? she ses, —sitting there with a big long face on you—

I just ignored her. I could've fought back cos I was strong again now, but like I say, I had better things to worry about now.

She didn't take the hint.

—Are you yapping again, are you? she ses. —Is your wee mate trying to stop you from crying again?

That was as far as she got. Nicola was up and out of her chair and squaring up. I jumped up as well for backup.

—WOULD YOU EVER SHUT UP! Nicola screamed. She was probably all stressed out cos of you know what.

The class went quiet. Kelly looked shocked, but then she tried to recover.

—What's your problem, Cummings, she said, —sticking up for your girlfriend are you—

And Nicola headbutted her. Better, far better than she'd done the last time, and she broke Kelly's nose.

17.

Cos of what happened next everything else happened later. Me and the rest of the class, except Nicola, gawped and looked bugeyed at Kelly. She was on the ground screaming like a tortured dog and holding her hands to her nose. It was pishing blood, I've never seen that much blood come out of one punch.

But I moved quick. I could hear feet running down the corridor and I knew the UN was on its way. Nicola was dead now, she was suspended at least, and she was pregnant and in loads of shit already. I thought quick, and I moved quick. I could see the door opening, and I jumped up and grabbed Kelly by the hair and I kicked her in the head.

18.

I did it on purpose, see, to back Nicola up. If she hadn't of been pregnant I probably wouldn't have thought of it, but I didn't want her having all this on her own as well as being up the duff. (And there was a big part of me pretty happy to kick Kelly in the head anyway.) I wasn't trying to be tough or noble, it's just that Nicola's my best mate and you stick up for your mates no matter what. So I did it.

It's all a bit blurred after I did it, it was like being in a dream. I remember Hornball being totally, completely, bugeyed at the Unfolded Scene. He couldn't even speak at first. He moved over to us in slow motion. I could see his mouth moving, all slow, but I couldn't hear what he was saying cos Kelly was still screaming and cos my ears were thumping my heartbeat. There was a buzz as well, I think it was the rest of the class, the chickenshit arselickers, all shouting to Hornball what'd happened so they didn't get blamed on it.

Then we were out of the classroom, and like I was walking on someone else's legs. Then we were in Reid's office. He was shouting as well, but I don't remember what he said cos it was just noise. I still felt like I was in a dream. I looked down at the floor and Nicola had blood on her skirt. There was a wee bit splattered on her trainers as well.

Then Reid went out. I wanted to say something to Nicola but Hornball was still there. I think he started shouting again but I don't remember that either.

Then Reid came back in. He had something, envelopes I think, in his hand. He put them on his desk.

Then I heard the word 'police'.

I came out of the dream. I looked up.

—And your parents are on their way as well, Reid was saying.

As well, I thought, as well as what? Cos I'd heard 'police' so that must mean he'd called the peelers. For a fight! He needed to wise up.

Kelly's nose had been broke, but. I'd heard it crunch.

I was getting scared now, I was more scared than I'd ever been. I wasn't scared of the peelers cos of the peelers, but cos of Paul. I was a dick for booting Kelly. You stick up for your mates, OK, but you don't need to get killed for doing it—

We were took out to the corridor to wait for the peelers and our mas and das. They left us on our own, cos beside Reid's office it's a glass wall into the secretary's office and Hornball said to her Keep an eye on these two. Then he went back to the form room, and at least I can be pleased to say that I haven't seen the baldy bastard since. And even happier to say that that's Colabottlehead's Part In This Tale over as well.

Nicola was crying. She was letting on she wasn't, there was just wee tears coming and every wee bit she moved her hand up and wiped them away. But she was crying all the same.

—Lisa, she ses.

But that's as far as she got cos there was her da coming up the corridor.

He only works down the road so he would've got there before her ma who works in Lurgan and would've had to get the bus. He looked like he'd ran the whole way, and he looked ripping. I'd never seen his face like that, Nicola's ma and da are sound usually.

He fired up to us. I could feel Nicola shrinking beside me.

He stood right in front of her. He said,

—You're expelled. Do you know that?

He hit her.

Not hard, not vicious. Definitely not like Paul hits me, it wasn't even a punch. It was the back of his hand on the back of her head, a knuckle rap, and it didn't even look like it hurt that much. But I was near as shocked as Nicola. I don't think her ma or da's ever hit her in her life.

He went into Reid's office and Nicola let herself out. It was a big shaky breath and it turned into a sob at the end. She couldn't stop it now, and I don't blame her, she was too shocked at her da.

—Lisa, she ses again.

I don't know if what she wanted to say then was what she was going to say before her da got to her. But she said,

—C'mon, I'm going, c'mon just go—

Not 'run away' she said, cos that was for kids and we weren't kids. But I knew what she meant. And I didn't even have to think about it. When she said it I got a thrill in my stomach, I'd been planning to try again since I was twelve and now I'd have someone with me.

I'd've tried again anyway I think, cos we were expelled

!

and maybe arrested and that meant I was double dead. But now Nicola was coming with me so it was like I was lying in bed making it up just how I wanted it.

We talked out of the sides of our mouths, like we were in a jail film. —How can we get out, I said.

—We'll just go, if she sees us we'll run—

That could work, cos getting into shit didn't matter now. But still —

—I've no money, have you any money?

—There'll be some in the house, Nicola ses, —if my ma and da are up here there'll be no-one in—

Oh god this was danger, and my stomach near fell out at the thought of it. I looked at Nicola and I knew she felt the same.

But there was nothing else we could do. We stood there for a bit, and we kept looking at Kennedy typing away in her office, and we knew we had to go now, at once, right away, before Nicola's ma or my ma and Paul got here. Finally I said, —C'mon, cos I knew we just had to do it and it didn't even matter, did it, if she did see us?

We slid down the corridor. When you get to the end of the corridor you can turn right for Kennedy's office and the main door, or left for the science block. We had to go left even though it was miles to the side door that way cos otherwise Kennedy would see us. We went left. My shoulders sharpened and my back pricked and I felt like I was waiting for someone to shoot me. If she looked up she'd shout.

She must've looked up, cos she did shout. It was like a gunshot, or maybe a whipcrack, and I near fell over with the fear of it. I could hear her door opening, and I knew that in a second Reid's door would open as well, and him and Nicola's da would come after us, and—

—RUN! I shouted at Nicola

and we did.

We ran panicked and fast, the way you think you're going to fall. We ran for ages but it probably wasn't, and we found the side door and we opened it and we ran out and down the hill and all the way to Nicola's house.

Nicola's hands were shaking so much she couldn't get the key in the door for ages, and I was near sick by now with the fear. Someone was going to come after us, Reid would drive down from the school, and maybe it would be easier on my stomach and my heart just to sink to the ground and wait for them.

Nicola had the door open. We poured into the hall. She put the snib on, good thinking that Nic, and then we didn't know what to do. We had to be quick so much that we couldn't think.

—What—

My voice wouldn't work. I swallowed nothing and I tried again.

—What do we need?

—Um, Nicola said.

—*Quick*, Nicola!

I was thinking again now. We had to be fast, fast, cos I bet in a couple of minutes Nicola's da and Reid would twig where we'd run to and they'd arrive at the door. Or else Nicola's ma would come in to get something before she went up to see Reid—

Nicola was still stood there.

—Get a bag, I said, —we need some stuff—

Our schoolbags were still in Reid's office, and for a sec I thought shit, my smokes are in mine so my ma'll find them. Then I near laughed. But Nicola sort of shook herself, and she moved. She ran upstairs two each and I ran into the kitchen and started hauling open the cupboards.

It's probably what those people feel you see on the telly, the ones who've only got one minute or whatever to run round a supermarket and get as much stuff as they can. If I had of had time I would've picked good stuff, proper stuff that didn't weigh too much and didn't need heating up. But I just had to grab. I got beans, a tin of spaghetti, a tin of peaches and some tomato soup. But I couldn't see anything else, it was all stuff like flour and ketchup and pasta sauce and cornflakes. There was half a loaf of bread and I took that, and two apples cos they were sitting there and cos there was nothing else.

Nicola was back, with a wee army rucksack. I threw the tins into it.

She was dragging a chair across the floor. I didn't have to ask, I knew where her ma kept the bills money. I held my breath and she looked in the tin.

—Ten, she said.

Well, it was better than nothing.

There was a box of smokes of her da's sitting on the living room table and she took them. I said she should take some makeup of her ma's from the bathroom as well, in case we had to look older or different. Then she had to wipe all the messages off her mobile and leave it on the table cos phones can be traced. They all had to be done, but I was near wetting myself with stress and every time I heard a car I thought I was going to faint.

We near forgot about clothes, we were still in our school uniforms and bit of a giveaway that would've been. We ran up to Nicola's room. We were going to get caught. We wrenched our clothes off down to bras, knickers and tights, and shows how urgent this was that we didn't even get scundered.

Nicola pulled on her combats and a T shirt and a jumper, and she stuffed a pair of jeans and another T shirt into the rucksack. Then she gave me jeans and a jumper, and even though we were in a panic and a rush I noticed she gave me the jeans her ma had bought her in the Primark sale, the ones that were far too big on her. They fit me fine.

It took me three goes to button my coat but then we were ready and Nicola opened the door. She had her house keys in her hand, and she closed the door behind us and then she opened the letterbox and she dropped the keys through it onto the wooden floor. I remember thinking that the noise was like a jail door being slammed behind us. It was final.

19.

Then we realised we didn't have a clue where to go. We'd ran out of Nicola's house, and into another estate, and under a bridge where it would have to be a miracle to be found there. —So where? I said to Nicola, and she said she didn't know, and then we just sat there for a bit smoking and not saying anything else.

We thought Belfast in the end, cos really there was nowhere else. I would've preferred Dublin but we weren't going to get there on a tenner, and there was no way we could hitch cos we didn't know where to hitch from and cos we couldn't stand on the main road waiting for Nicola's da anyway.

It was sinking in a bit for Nicola, I could tell, and I wanted to get her away before she changed her mind. So I got us to the bus stop.

We waited about half an hour for the bus, it was terrible. Every car that came past we didn't know who it was, but we couldn't run from the bus stop cos that'd look too suss. So we had to stand there and brick it, and every time the car went past I thought that's it, that has to be the last one, I can't do this again. But then there the bus was, a blue and white horse trundling down the road towards us and I near wet myself again with relief.

My stomach clenched one last time when Nicola was paying us onto the bus, I thought someone was going to jump out from behind the bus stop and shout, Here get back here now.

But then there we were, on the bus and in the back seat, laughing and near crying from the relief of it. We were going, we were running away, we were off, and when I stopped laughing and I leaned against the window with my mouth sore my brain kept singing We're off to see the wizard the wonderful wizard of Oz.

Part II
Us

1.

On the bus we talked about Colabottlehead first. Nicola was delighted with me booting her in the head.

—On top of a broke nose as well—

I'd had to kick her in the head and not the face, but. I couldn't've kicked someone in the face who had a broken nose, not even her. It'd make me be sick.

I said to Nicola and she said Yeah.

—Imagine the sound it'd make—

—Did you hear the sound of it anyway, when you headbutted her—

We tried to say what sound it'd been like, our English teacher would've been proud of us. Like when you snap a chicken bone, Nicola ses, but I didn't agree with her, it was too obvious. It'd been more like when you stand on a beetle, only the sound had been faster and wetter cos there was all the blood. Nicola said I was talking shite, but I let her have a victory cos I knew deep down I was right and cos I was too happy to care.

We talked a bit about how Reid and Hornball would've cracked up when they heard we'd ran out of the school. Kennedy was probably going to get sacked for it, Nicola said. We didn't talk about Nicola's da hitting her. We laughed. My heart kept jumping, then sort of blossoming, it felt like it'd opened and gone all warm. I wanted to shout and laugh, I felt like I was flying. I was getting away from Paul, from everything, and I had Nicola with me.

2.

We were starving. It was getting dark, getting tea time, and we were in the city centre, wandering about cos we didn't have a clue what else to do. We stood across the road from a food stand and we watched a skinny wee kid fry burgers and sausages and onions. We were starving. £2 the cardboard sign against the ketchup bottle said.

Nicola ses,

—Do you want a hot dog?

We only had a fiver left after paying two halves on the bus and that was all our money left in the world. But we'd get some more money tomorrow, it was what running away, leaving, was all about. Yeah, I said.

—D' want onions? the wee kid ses, and we said Yeah, and we drenched the hot dogs in ketchup and mustard. I can still taste that hot dog, it was perfect. I was so hungry and my stomach was so empty I could feel the first bite, the first hot lump of it, go all the way down and into me. I thought, Why I can't be skinny, cos if I was I'd eat stuff like this all the time. It made me sad even though I was happy.

We walked around a bit after the hot dogs, but it was only cos we still didn't know what to do. It was really dark now and we had to find somewhere to sleep and I didn't know how to. I'd never got this far when I'd run away before. I'd just thought you just found somewhere.

We were sleeping outside. In February, it's like I just realised it. I shivered a bit, but not cos of the cold. We were homeless. You could freeze to death sleeping outside in February.

Nicola knew too we had to find somewhere, but she was letting on she didn't. I said to her.

—Where, it's freezing! she said.

I didn't know did I, how would I. Just in out of the cold, an alley or behind a big building or something.

I told her. She looked like she was going to say something, but she didn't.

We walked we didn't know where. We should try and find the student area cos then maybe we'd get asked in to a party, Nicola said. But we didn't have a clue where it was or how to get there. So we just walked.

It got bad pretty fast once we left the city centre. We were in estates now, and there was flags and murals everywhere, and we thought we were going to get killed. We knew about Belfast. If you wander into the wrong area people beat you up and kill you. Well we'll just let on we're from this bit then, I said, but Nicola said no, they ask whereabouts round here, and who do you know, so they can tell if you're spoofing or not—

I was jangly now, I was seeing people in the shadows and I thought if we didn't find somewhere soon I was going to have a heart attack from the tension. It was like when I was waiting for Paul to get home when my ma was going to tell him I'd done something, my hands were sweaty and my throat was dry and I kept jumping at noises. The darker it got the further we got into the badlands and the more nervous me and Nicola got. —We'll stop at the first OK place, all right, Nicola said, and I said Yeah.

We were going up a hill and there was flags leering over the top of it, and I thought no, I can't go into another estate, my head'll not take it. But there was a garage halfway up the hill and Nicola said to c'mon stop here, it'd do rightly, and again I said Yeah.

It wasn't too bad at all, at least not for sleeping outside. Round the back of the garage there was a wee alley, and there was two big industrial bins at the end of it that blocked us off from the road if we sat behind them. The ground wasn't too bad either, a couple of big puddles but mostly dry.

—I'm knackered, Nicola said.

So was I. I thought of this morning, getting up in my ma's house and going to school, and it seemed like ages ago. It felt like miles away as well, I mean more miles than it was.

Nicola put her bag on the ground and sat on it and leaned against the wall. I'd no bag to sit on, but I looked in one of the bins and there was a flattened cardboard box that wasn't too bogging. I put it on the ground and sat on it and leaned against the wall.

Nicola lit us a smoke each and we smoked them. We didn't talk. It was too cold. We sat not speaking and waiting for the daylight.

Hours later Nicola was asleep. We sat for ages not talking but I knew from her breathing she was as awake as me, but then I knew she was asleep. Jammy bitch.

I wouldn't sleep, I knew it. So I just sat there and listened to the night. There was lots of shouting, and cars, but then it went all quiet and it was spooky. It was like a grave. It started to freak me out cos all I could hear was Nicola's breathing and me shivering, so I got up and walked about a wee bit. Then for a bit there were cars, and they were roaring and screeching down the road, they must've been joyriders. Then it went quiet again.

I was freezing. I sat with my head huddled into the collar of my coat and I waited for morning. I tried not to think.

3.

—We'll nick some tablets, Nicola said, —and sell them and let on they're Es—

We were skint now. Nicola'd woke up at about six and we'd had the beans and the spaghetti cold with the half loaf of bread cos we couldn't wait to make it last. Then when the garage opened we spent our last quid on two wee sausage rolls cos we were both freezing, I couldn't even feel my feet. We only had the tin of peaches and the tin of tomato soup left, and twelve smokes, and that was it.

We were in the bogs round the back of some caff. We'd went in cos of fixing our hair, not cos we were being bigheaded bitches but cos we didn't want to make it totally obvious to everyone that we didn't have a home to go to. Nicola put a bit of makeup on, and I tried to as well but it went all streaky so I had to wipe it off and feel depressed. Now we were sitting on the sinks and we were smoking.

—Well, for food we can just nick things out of shops, I said.

—And what if we get caught?

I hadn't even thought about that cos I was just so happy to get away. But if we got caught everything would be over, we were dead. But we had to eat, and we'd no money. I felt black panic.

Nicola said,

—And there's smokes as well, we can't nick them after these ones are finished—

—Gimme one, someone said.

It scared the shite out of us, cos we hadn't even noticed anyone come in. We whipped round, and there was a girl stood there. She looked like she was trying to act all hard, so we put on snattery faces and looked back.

She was wee, and skinny, about eleven or twelve. Younger than Paddy's Marie, anyway. But she was wearing makeup, and big dangly gold hoop earrings, and a Nike fleece, and tracksuit bottoms and trainers. She had a carrier bag on her arm.

—Gimme one, she said again.

Nicola recovered first. —No—

—Go on—

—No!

—I'll give you a drink if you give me a smoke, the girl said. She unzipped her fleece a wee bit and showed us a bottle of vodka.

Nicola's eyes lit up. As much as mine did, probably. So she gave the girl a smoke and the girl slid the bottle of vodka out from under her fleece and over to us. It was cheap vodka, raw, loads left. Nicola swigged at it and passed me the bottle. I took a huge mouthful, held it, swigged, and I swear to god it was the first time I'd been warm since yesterday. I held the bottle, cos I was hoping to get another swig. The girl looked at it but she didn't put out her hand to take it back, so I took another gulp and I handed the bottle to Nicola. After she took another swig the girl did take the bottle back. She took three swallows of it (her mouth must've been on fire) and put it back in her fleece.

—So you've run away, she said. Her accent was terrible, it could've cut bricks.

—No we haven't, Nicola said.

—Aye right—

—We haven't, I said, —and it's none of your business anyway—

—Only asking, the girl said.

She finished her smoke. She looked at mine but I'd near finished it so I took the last draw of it and butted it down the sink.

Then she said,

—It's just that if you have, you can hang about with us if want—

A gang! A lawless underworld gang! I've always wanted to be in one of them. Living on our own, and not having to listen to mas or teachers—

But Nicola was all paranoid. She jumped in before I could say Bloody hell yes please.

—Who's us? she said.

—Just us—

—Yeah, but who's that?

—Us! the girl said, sounding a bit pissed off, and I wished Nicola'd leave off with the questions, we could find out who us was once we got there and saw them. —Us! Me and my mates!

—Yeah, but—

—Look, the girl said, —do yis want to come back or do yis not?

I know Nicola was dying to go, Come back where? but at least she had the sense to keep her trap shut this time. I thought she was being stupid. This girl seemed OK, and even if her mates weren't we could just say we had to go somewhere else. And she obviously knew what she was doing and how to get on with no money and nowhere to sleep. I could see into her carrier bag and there was shower gel and toothpaste and a rag of towel in it. She must've been coming into the bogs to get washed, same as me and Nicola, and that meant she'd run away as well.

—What're yis called? she said. Her accent made it sound like she'd kill us once she found out.

—Nicola—

—Lisa—

—I'm called Karen, she said. —Gimme another smoke Nicola, would ?

4.

It took us ages to get to where she said her mates were. She said it was a bit of a walk, but we'd've been quicker if she hadn't kept nicking stuff from shops along the way. It was only wee stuff she was nicking, crisps and smellies and makeup, but she wouldn't let me and Nicola come in with her. She said security guards always watched young ones if there was more than one or two of them.

—Probably scared we'll cramp her style, Nicola said. (Nicola was a bit pissed off. I don't know why. I was in great form, we were getting sorted out, we weren't going to starve, and Karen was brilliant, the sort of person anyone'd want to hang about with. I don't know what Nicola's problem was.)

So anyway, it took us ages getting out of the city centre. And then we walked for ages, eating crisps, and we could've been anywhere and I started thinking Karen wasn't so brilliant at all, she was going to lead us up some dark wee alley somewhere and murder us for our peaches and tomato soup. Cos of not sleeping last night I was near swaying on my feet I was so tired, and I started thinking if we didn't get to wherever soon I was going to fall over.

—Are we near there, Nicola snapped at Karen.

—Keep your knickers on! Karen said back. I looked at her face when she said that, and I thought, OK, I wouldn't fancy my chances against you in a fight even if you are so titchy—

Nicola felt the same maybe; at least, she didn't say anything. But she put a huffy gob on her, and there was a big, long, awkward silence. We trudged on.

Then the next thing was we were going up a hill and Karen pushed the sleeves of her fleece up cos of being too warm (how anyone could be warm in this ballfreezing hole I don't know, but maybe Belfast people were freaks). Anyway, she pushed her sleeves up and Nicola suddenly nudged me so hard I squeaked.

—What? Karen said from in front of us.

—Nothing! Nicola said, so fast she near choked on it, and near choked on trying not to make it sound snattery, cos I got the feeling that if Karen had to say Keep your knickers on to Nicola again, Nicola'd be wearing the road.

Karen kept walking though, she mustn't've thought Nicola was being snattery. So Nicola nudged me again, and then she nodded over at Karen's arms. We could see the bottom of them, up to her elbows, and they were funny looking cos there was loads of red lines on them. They were scars it looked like. And they were done careful, at least they looked like they were done on purpose, cos they were all the same size and the same distance apart as well. There was about twenty of them on each arm. They didn't look new, but they were deep in her skin, and they were red and raw and angry looking.

Maybe her da's a nut as well, I wanted to say. But I didn't.

She hadn't got those falling through a window though. I wondered who'd done it to her.

Nicola was still jerking her head towards Karen's arms. She was trying to tell me something but I couldn't figure out what. I shook my head at her and she looked pissed off.

Karen turned round.

My stomach jumped. But she didn't catch on, cos Nicola had copped on fast and changed her face. Karen said,

—We're near here—

The top of the hill had an estate on it. It was pretty much the same as home, cos it had dog shite and rubbish and snotty nosed wee kids. But here there was more flags and there was wall murals and painted kerbs as well.

There was loads of people about. Especially kids, they only looked about six but like they'd kill you soon as look at you. They were all skinny and freckled and wearing sweatshirts and tracksuit bottoms. Their mas thundered down the pavements behind them with bags from the shop.

Karen didn't give us any time to look round us. There was an offy across the road with barbed wire fencing and barricaded steel doors, and she went over to it with us behind her. There was an alley beside it. It was bogging and it smelt really strong of piss. Like I say, same as home.

We stepped past puddles and old nappies and went into the alley. There was a steel ladder running up the wall. Maybe it was a fire escape, I don't know, and why does it matter, shut up head.

—C'mon, Karen said.

She started to go up the ladder. Me and Nicola looked at each other, and we decided without saying anything we might as well give it a go, just to see. So we went up the ladder behind Karen. I went first.

At the top Karen was standing on a sort of balcony, well a steel platform sort of thing. It was covered in butts and puddled plastic bags. There wasn't enough room for me or Nicola to stand on it as well, so I hung off the top of the ladder and Nicola waited under me. We'd soon see now if we were going to get killed or not.

I looked down at Nicola. She was a bit pale, maybe it'd made her tired going up the ladder. But I was probably pale too I suppose.

She grinned up at me and I grinned back and we waited.

There was a door at end of the balcony thing and Karen knocked on it. She knocked two, then three, then two. A secret code! I wanted to say to Nicola but I didn't in case Karen heard me.

And then suddenly I was shitting it. Not about maybe getting killed, but cos I'd just thought someone would be coming to the door, there'd be people here I didn't know. People just don't seem to like me when they first meet me, I don't know why. Especially fellas, but I do know with them. If there were fellas in here they'd just take one look at me and decide I wasn't worth bothering with, cos I was ugly. I know the look.

Anyway, the door opened above us. It was a fella, and by now I was shitting myself so much I near fell off the ladder. I hate being shy. Nearly as much as I hate not being skinny. (If I'd one wish though, I'd pick to be skinny, cos if you're skinny and shy people think it's cute, but if you're fat and ugly and shy they just say What a dick.)

Anyway. Karen went in through the door, but she didn't say C'mon. And the fella didn't either, he just stood there and stared at us and didn't say anything. It was terrible, me and Nicola hanging off the ladder not knowing if we were allowed in or not and this fella standing staring down at us. Then Karen came back, and she looked through the door, and she said,

—Are you coming or what? so we went up the rest of the ladder.

But the fella was still stood on the balcony, even though there wasn't enough room for all of us. Me and Nicola had to push past him a bit to get in through the door, and he still didn't move. He had one of those rough holey faces people have when they've had load of spots years ago, and he looked old, about twenty-five. He was a bit creepy I thought.

We got inside. We were in a hall and there was four white doors leading off it. But we didn't know what one Karen'd gone through. We stood there like dicks, and the fella was still on the balcony with the door open. But then we heard Karen, she shouted Mackers! and the fella finally stopped gawking at us and he came in and went through one of the white doors.

Me and Nicola stood there like lemons. Maybe we were meant to go after him, but then maybe him and Karen would be pissed off if we caught on to them plotting our bloody deaths.

—Did you see her arms! Nicola said.

I think she'd been dying to say it for the last ten minutes.

I didn't really want to talk about Karen's arms, cos she had scars so what, what was the big deal and cos maybe she could hear us from the room she was in. I didn't want to talk about anything in case there was someone listening.

Nicola said,

—I hope it's all right—

To be here she meant, and funny she should say that just as I was thinking the weapons were being shouldered in the room in front of us. I didn't say anything.

Nicola said,

—It's just her arms, did you see them—

I didn't get this obsession with Karen's arms. And I was scared someone could hear us. But Nicola was on a roll. I hisswhispered at her,

—What about them!

—She—

Nicola let on with her hand that she was slashing her arm. I looked at her. She tutted at me. She said,

—She did it herself Lisa! Are you thick?

I was. She had. I took a beamer.

Then I twigged on to what Nicola meant. Karen seemed all right but maybe she wasn't. How could someone be all right if they did that on themselves, why would you do that?

Maybe we could open the balcony door dead quiet and get down the fire escape again. But if they caught us—

One of the white doors opened. My stomach jumped and then curled.

Karen said,

—Are yis not coming in?

like we were at her ma's house for tea or something, like it hadn't been clearer than vodka her and the creepy fella'd been talking about us.

So anyway we went in. It was a living room, a big one. The walls were white wallpaper and there were mattresses and couch cushions on the floor and a SuperSer in the middle of the room. There was an upside down milk crate with a wee stereo sat on top of it and a goldfish in a bowl on a shelf. And there was loads of rubbish – blue offy bags and empty beer tins and smoke boxes and butts and chippy bags.

At first I thought it was clothes on the floor but then they moved and said, —Close the door, it's freezing—

—That's Bonanz, Karen said about the pile of clothes on the floor.

—And that's Mackers, she said about the creepy fella.

Mackers, the human gorilla, just looked at us again from under his big eyebrow. But Bonanz put a hand out of his blanket and waved it around at us.

—Hiya! I said. Like a dick.

—All right, Nicola said, like a normal person.

Karen sat down on one of the couch cushions and she pulled the bottle of vodka out of her fleece. The Mackers one sat down and started making a roll-up. Me and Nicola stood there, still lemony. We weren't waiting to be asked to sit down, cos this wasn't high tea, but we didn't want to just take it for granted in case we weren't staying, weren't allowed to stay. But then Karen said, —Here Nicola, gimme one more smoke and you me and Lisa'll split the rest of this voddy—

So we sat down. And that was it. We were in.

5.

She wasn't twelve at all, she was fifteen. She had a foster ma and da but she'd run away from them three months ago. —Well, ten weeks, she said. She'd run away loads of times before but this was the longest she'd never been caught. She'd had foster parents since she was ten.

She hadn't got caught this time she said cos she was on a different estate, all the other times she'd run away she'd had to stick near to home cos of her mates being there and cos of needing money and food. Me and Nicola were a bit chuffed when she said that, cos we'd come thirty miles and we knew no-one'd ever find us in this flat. We didn't let on we were chuffed but we thought it. Maybe we'd be OK at this.

That first night was weird. I'd never felt so shy in my life I don't think, but I was excited as well. Me and Karen and Nicola sat and drank the voddy and smoked the rest of Nicola's da's cigarettes. Bonanz stayed under his blanket and Mackers sat and smoked and didn't talk to us. But he was listening to us, I could tell by the way his head was. I tried not to talk much.

There was a knock on the door outside, the proper knock, the code. Mackers looked at Karen and she got up to answer it. Me and Nicola waited, and Karen came back in with another girl. The girl looked at me and Nicola, and me and Nicola looked back at her. (It's a hard expression to do. You don't want to look too snattery in case someone jumps on your head, but you don't want anyone thinking they can take the piss out of you either. I'm good at it now, but it takes loads of practice.)

The girl stopped looking at us, and she looked at Karen. Karen said to her, —Julie, c'mere a wee minute—

And they went out into the hall and me and Nicola sat there, miserably sure they were going to kick us out. This Julie woman looked about eighteen, hard as bricks, totally in charge of the squat or at least what girls were in it. We waited.

There didn't seem to be an argument going on outside, or else they were whispering. We waited. The door opened.

Karen said,

—So. Are you two stickin around for a bit then?

My heart swelled again, even more than on the bus. This was brilliant.

—Aye, all right, Nicola said, pleased but sounding cool about it.

—If you don't mind! I said, sounding like a dick once more.

The Julie person looked at me. I felt like a smurf.

—Nah, we don't *mind*, she said, —it's easier to get stuff if there's more of us—

Now I felt like a small smurf. But stuff it, we had somewhere to stay and the main thing was that Paul's face was fading.

The Julie one had brought food with her, a KFC bargain bucket so even though she didn't know me and Nicola were going to be in the squat there was still enough left over for some chips and a wee bit of chicken each. She had smokes as well and she flashed them, and once when Karen reached over and got one without being flashed Julie didn't say anything.

Mackers said,

—Any drink, Julie? and she said,

—No, I was just nicking today so there's not enough—

She couldn't nick a KFC bargain bucket, and if she could she could nick out of an offy as well. I didn't get it. Nick what?

Karen saw my face.

—We lift wallets, she said.

When they needed stuff like toiletries or some types of food they sometimes nuck them directly from shops, but if they needed other stuff like KFC or smokes or booze they lifted wallets and handbags. Wallets were the easiest. You had to look out for the wallet in the back pocket of their jeans and bump into them and take it, crowded places like markets were good. Pubs were the best, Karen said, really crowded and people too drunk to look after their wallets right, but sometimes the bouncers wouldn't let you in even with false ID and you had to be careful with CCTV as well.

Handbags could be good cos you normally got a mobile as well but you had to know what type of strap broke or how people carried them and what ones you could snap off their shoulder. Karen had dislocated someone's shoulder once. You ran past them and grabbed the bag as you were running, only this time it hadn't come off and Karen was still running so the person got their shoulder twisted and they fell.

—Did you get the bag? I said.

—Nah, couldn't go back, you should've heard the screams of her—

This was class.

They nuck other stuff out of shops, clothes and perfume and electric carving knives and all sorts of stuff. They had to watch for the cameras but they were good at nicking and they never got caught. There was a fella on the estate bought stuff off them or swapped them for cheap smokes.

Mackers gave a big huffy sigh, and he got up and went out. Don't worry about him, Karen said.

But he came back half an hour later with drink, a twenty four bottle crate of beer. They were only wee bottles, French I think, but there was enough for a couple for me and Nicola. We didn't want to take one at first, and we weren't offered, but then Karen said, —Can Nicola and Lisa have one, Mackers? and he grunted Aye.

Julie and Karen taught us how to nick stuff. Karen went into one of the other rooms and came back with wallets and handbags. We nuck all these, she said, and I thought it was stupid to leave them in the squat in case the peelers raided it, but of course I didn't say anything. Anyway, Karen put one of the bags on her shoulder and got me and Nicola in turns to run past and grab it off her. I was feeling really shy, cos everyone was watching us, and Karen made me do it ten times cos she said I wasn't doing it right and I was near crying with the embarrassment of it. But after a bit the two beers hit me so it didn't matter as much.

—That's it, Karen said.

Then she stuck one of the wallets in the pocket of her tracksuit bottoms and we had to take it out without her feeling it. It was brilliant, she was really funny, letting on to be looking in shop windows and talking in a posh voice Hmm, what a wonderful television, darling, it would look simply marvellous in the east wing drawing room wouldn't it? She stuck her arse out so me and Nicola could get the wallet easy every time.

—You're like Fagan, I said to Karen, cos she reminded me of Oliver Twist. But she didn't know who I meant, and she gave me a look like I was mad, and so did Julie and then so did Nicola.

The four white doors in the corridor were: living room, bedroom, bedroom, bathroom. There was no water from the taps but the bog flushed OK. The bathroom was minging, I never sat down on the seat on the toilet and I'm not usually fussy about stuff like that. There was hardly ever bog roll as well.

When everyone said they were going to bed we found out where they all slept. Bonanz stayed under his pile of blankets in the living room, and Julie went into one of the bedrooms. Mackers went into the other one and then me and Nicola arranged sofa cushions and blankets on the floor. I thought Karen was going to sleep on the living room floor as well, but then she went out and one of the bedroom doors shut so she was sleeping with either Julie or Mackers. Scary thoughts both.

I was scared to get up the next day. I was awake really early, way before everyone else, but I was too scared and shy to get out from under the blankets so I let on I was still sleeping. I heard people leaving.

Then the living room door opened and Karen came in.

—Do you fancy a walk to the shop, Mackers gave me some money for breakfast—

It was Mackers she was with! I near think Julie would've been better.

Nicola was still asleep and we left her. She needed her sleep though of course I didn't say anything to Karen about that she did or why.

We went to a shop up the road and Karen bought ten Mayfair and four bacon and egg rolls and some Coke, and we went back. They were lovely, them rolls, we ate them sitting on the floor of the squat, me and Karen and Nicola and Bonanz, drinking Coke from the bottle and wiping the grease from our fingers on our trousers.

—I'm away, Bonanz said, and he was.

—Right, Karen ses, —are yis ready?

6.

She was great at nicking, Karen, she hadn't been lying when she said about never getting caught. She let me and Nicola come into the shops at the same time as her this time, but we had to let on we weren't with her. We watched her going round the shop. Even though we knew she was nicking we couldn't see her doing it, she disappeared the stuff too fast. I thought of me and Nicola lifting the Man U shirt and I was scundered for us.

She walked out not looking at us. We waited a bit til we thought we were doing it right, then we followed her to round the corner. She had deodorant, chocolate and batteries. And a purse.

Me and Nicola near fell over.

—Where'd you get that?

—From some old doll looking at cabbages—

She held the purse up and admired it. It was red and scuffed, with a clasp. An oldlady purse.

Nicola said,

—She'll know, she'll cop on when she goes to pay—

—She'll think she's lost it in the shop and she'll get everyone to look for it, and they'll take about an hour, and by the time they twig on someone's lifted it we'll be at home—

—What about the security cameras, Nicola said. She said it a bit snattery I thought.

—There isn't none in that bit of the shop—

—How do you know?

Still snattery.

Karen got annoyed.

—Cos do you think I'd nick some old doll's purse without knowing there was no cameras about?

I could near hear Nicola thinking, Well um maybe. But she had the sense to keep her mouth shut.

Karen was still annoyed though. I didn't blame her. Course I'd stick up for Nicola if it came to it, but it was stupid to slabber like that, it was too early yet. We'd only known Karen a day, and she'd been nothing but sound to us.

She counted the money in the oldlady purse and there was twelve quid and some money off coupons she threw away. She said to Nicola,

—So. What're you two getting?

—What do mean?

—I mean *getting*, she said, —what're you *getting*, for the *flat*—

I could've killed Nicola. Even though we'd done all the Consider Yourself stuff last night I didn't feel near confident enough yet to just go up to someone and nick their wallet. But if we didn't the squat might be finished for us. But if we got caught—

Karen's mobile beeped a text. Saved by the bell. Time for Nicola to wise up or Karen to calm down, and then maybe we'd be saved.

But no. Karen read the text said Julie was getting the food in for the night, so the three of us had to get the smokes and booze.

—I'll get the smokes with this money here, so you two have to get the booze, she said.

Maybe she was wanting us to get caught cos she didn't like us.

I said,

—But we can't nick out of an offy, we'll get caught—

—Have to nick a wallet then, Karen said.

—That's too hard too, Nicola said. She near spat it.

—Didn't me and Julie show yis how last night?! Karen shouted.

I felt like standing in between them like one of the Scousers and going Calm dahn, calm dahn. Nicola was going to get us kicked out of the squat. I didn't know what was wrong with her.

—Are yis chickens? Karen said.

—No!

—Then what's your problem?

She said it quiet, but there was blood in the air. I could near see it.

Nicola said,

—I'm not getting caught and brought back home by the peelers just so you can all have some drink!

—Weren't you drinking our drink yesterday, and didn't you get food! Karen shouted.

Then she said,

—Peelers! Peelers! Big bloody wow about the peelers!

We didn't say anything, we couldn't. Karen was sound and we'd landed on our feet at the squat, but it didn't mean we'd been stupid enough to say anything about why we were in Belfast. They knew we were from Craigavon, but that was only cos it was too hard to lie, anywhere we'd've mentioned could've had someone saying Hey my ma lives there, whereabouts round there are you from?

Nicola copped on to this, I could tell by the way her throat moved. She made herself swallow being angry and go all quiet and calm and reasonable instead. She said, —We just don't want to get caught, that's all—

I stuck up for her and I said, —We haven't been doing it as long as you have, we don't want to get caught the first time—

Nicola smirked a wee bit cos she knew my arselicky tactics. But Karen was still annoyed.

—Yis have to get something, she said.

7.

We were heroes. Maybe just for one day, but for this day at least cos we'd got a purse and there was eighty quid in it, eightybloodyquid. And it was so easy. We were both high still of how easy it was. We'd been going into a big shopping centre and then Karen had said —Look, so we looked, and we saw some woman who was going over to the trolleys, she'd took her purse out to get the pound out of it but then she'd just set her purse on top of her bag, she must've been going to close the bag after she got the trolley, anyway Karen said —Quick, go on! and she gave us a quid out of the cigarette money, and we went up and we let on we couldn't get the trolley working, and that was OK cos the woman couldn't either so we didn't look suspicious or anything, and then we got our trolley before her and Nicola said to her I hate these trolleys, and the woman said Yeah, and then while her and Nicola were both tutting at the trolleys I just reached out an inch and I lifted, hooked, her purse between my fingers. We abandoned trolley at the shop door and then we walked round the corner and then ran, and when we slowed down and looked in the purse there was eighty quid in it, eightybloodyquid.

Everyone cheered. Karen'd been trying to make me tell the story all night and I'd been too scundered. But I didn't mind now. I was going to tell everyone.

We came back like hunters. We couldn't even get up the ladder with all the booze bags, Karen had to go and get Mackers and Bonanz. Mackers was pissed off at having to get up but then when he saw the amount of the drink we'd got he was OK. We had two bottles of vodka and some Coke and four bottles of Bucky and some barrack busters and the rest in beer. Our arms were killed.

Bonanz wasn't pissed off at all. He just smiled at us and heaved the bags up. My stomach did funny.

—You fancy him, Nicola said later on.

—I do not, right—

I let on I was fixing the lace of my boot cos I didn't want to go into the squat with my face all red like a sunburnt tomato. But my reddener hadn't even stopped before it started again, cos when we got into the living room Mackers and Bonanz were handing out the drink and Karen was telling the story to the five other fellas sitting there, and when me and Nicola came in she give a big cheer. I stood there feeling like a dick and thinking my heat rash was going to come out and in front of fellas as well. But it was nice too in a way.

Julie was away for some food, and the SuperSer was on so it was warm, so I sat on the floor and opened a barrack buster and felt happy happy happy even though there was seven fellas in the room. This was a whole life I hadn't even knew existed, I hadn't had a clue people our age are able to live like this and make a go of it, get their own food and their own drink and live on their own without anyone annoying them. We're told so much about needing adults, but now I knew, we don't. It was brilliant.

8.

He was looking at me.

Out of the five other fellas three were Shrek One Two and Three, and one was OK, and one was scruffy and nice. It was the nice one who was looking at me and I burnt my mouth on the smoke when I saw him doing it. He smiled but not in a bad way. I smiled back, just a bit.

The OK one and the three Shreks were all looking at Nicola. Then the OK one looked at me. I went to smile at him, not cos I fancied him (like he'd look at me), but just cos I felt shy and wanted him to like me, but the look on his face stopped me, I couldn't read it. He was looking at me, but like he was trying to figure me out, but not in a nice way. I did smile at him, but he didn't smile back and I looked away before tears got hot in my eyes.

Then I thought, Stuff him. He didn't live here. I gave him a dirty look and went back to my cider.

Who cared about him anyway. I was pissed an hour later, it was funny, great. I hadn't even knew I was pissed til I tried to get up and my legs went Hah no. The only thing to grab onto to stop me falling on my arse was the OK one's dome, so I did and everyone laughed and after a bit he did as well.

I came back from the bog.

—I didn't even feel that cider hitting me, I said to Nicola. We were on the vodka now, sharing a bottle with Karen. No mixer but it didn't even burn now.

—It hasn't hit me yet! Nicola shouted, her face as red as Bonanz's Marlboro box and only wearing her vest top with her jeans and not her jumper cos she said she was too warm. The scruffy nice fella kept looking at her. I wished people'd look at me like that sometimes.

Shrek#1 was going round handing something out to people. I couldn't see what it was but looking at the happy mugs round me it must've been something good. So I kept gawking at him so he'd know I wanted whatever it was as well.

He came over to us anyway. Nicola gave him a Sorry do I know you? look but I smiled at him and said —Hiya! in that dimwit stupid way I can't seem to stop. He crouched down beside us and held out his hand.

—Here, get one of them down you—

He had aspirins or something in his hand, maybe if you took aspirins with drink it got you stoned. But the next second I could've kissed Karen cos she saved me making a dick of myself as usual. She was sitting beside us talking to Mackers and Bonanz, and when she saw Shrek#1's hand she went, Class! Es! and took two of them.

I'd've been laughed out of the place if I'd said Are they aspirins, and if I hadn't of been I would've left anyway. But Es! We were on the run criminals in a squat, drinking with money we'd nuck, and now there was drugs as well. I was so happy I near burst.

I took one of them from his palm and so did Nicola. If it'd been just me and her I would've been able to say What do you do, but I didn't want to ask in front of everyone. I gave Karen a sneaky look instead. She was still holding her Es cos she was waiting for Mackers and Bonanz to get theirs. They got two each as well.

Karen saw me looking and said, —Down in one?

She threw the Es into her mouth and took a big gulp of raw vodka. It might've been water for all the notice she took of it. I wanted to ask if me and Nicola needed two each as well but I didn't. I took the vodka off her, said Chin chin, and necked the E.

I didn't know what to expect. I thought once I'd took it I'd feel all happy and loved up and start hugging everyone, but I just felt the same. So I kept an eye on Karen to see what she was doing. But she just kept on talking away to Mackers and Bonanz with no bother on her at all. I waited for a bit. By the time I'd smoked a smoke there was no change in me, so I started talking to Nicola again and I forgot I'd took it.

The flat was bouncing. The music was on full and everyone was shouting and laughing. Me and Nicola were as well, I forgot feeling shy even though there were fellas here. I just felt brilliant. These people were brilliant and the flat was brilliant, we'd been dead lucky running into Karen yesterday like that. And we knew how to nick now, so we were independent, we could sort ourselves out if anything ever happened and we had to leave the flat. We weren't going to leave, but, this flat was great and I loved it.

I thought about Paul and how I'd never have to see his ugly face again, and my heart warmed up so much I could feel it in my feet. I wanted to cry I was so happy.

Karen came over.

—Are yis having a good night?

Me and Nicola shouted Yeah. I said to Karen thanks very much about bringing us here, and it was brilliant, and her and her mates were class. She laughed at me, but in a good way. —You're off your box wee girl, she said, and grabbed me and Nicola and gave us a hug.

Was I? Maybe? Maybe. Who cared. There was a song pushing itself out of the stereo, that one by Eminem that's in his film, I love it, I love Eminem even though I've none of his stuff cos my ma and Paul never give me any money, and for god's sake who cares about my bloody ma and bloody Paul.

—This song's class! I shouted to Karen, and she pulled me and Nicola up to dance. I couldn't believe I was dancing in front of people, especially fellas, but I knew I should and that the only thing wrong with me was that I was sometimes a bit too shy and sure there was nothing wrong with that. I was an OK person, I was a good person, I shouldn't be so hard on myself. There was nothing wrong with me.

I wasn't as cool as Nicola, though, or as nice looking, or as popular, but I didn't care. She was lucky and I loved being her mate. I was happy for her cos she was so cool and nice. I told her and she hugged me and still the music was in the room.

We danced for ages, I lost count. Then I looked round me and Karen was dancing with Mackers, and Nicola was dancing with the scruffy guy. And I'd been dancing like a dick, on my own, and I hadn't even noticed.

It was, really was, like a slap in the face. Or like a bucket of water being thrown over me. I looked round, all panicked. Julie was looking at me and so was Bonanz who was sitting beside her. I think they had their arms around each other, I'm not sure. It looked like it'd been decided ages ago, like a script, and it didn't surprise me at all.

I looked round some more. Everyone was looking at me. Has anyone got a smoke, I tried to say so I'd have something to say then something to do, but my mouth was dry and no words would move. I couldn't even hear the music, just the hammering in my head I always got when I'd made a real dick of myself. It was really loud.

I sat down fast. I knew I looked stupid doing it and like it mattered, like I cared, but it was worse standing up like a Billy no mates. There was a tin of beer beside me and I grabbed it not caring who owned it, if anyone mouthed about it I'd pour it over them, it was me who'd bought the bloody stuff in the first place. There was a Mayfair box as well, sitting a wee bit away from me, I'd have to stretch. I pretended not to look round me but I don't think anyone was looking any more. They probably knew I'd caught on so they were waiting til I wasn't looking up. I lifted the box, gently, softly between my fingers, the way I'd lifted the purse earlier, earlier was it today was it only today it couldn't be was it?

—Here, they're mine, someone said.

It was like getting slapped again. I was too scundered being caught lifting someone else's smokes that I couldn't say anything for a bit. Then I said —Sorry!, thinking that in a minute I was going to cry and that if I did me and Nicola would have to leave the squat for sure. I waited for a minute til I knew I wasn't going to, then I looked up. It was the OK fella. He didn't look too pissed off. Yet.

—Cheer up it might never happen, he said.

I hate that line but I didn't care. —I'm a dick, I said.

—What? Why?

He was nice, wanting to know. —I just am, I said.

—No you're not—

—I am, I was dancing there and no-one else was dancing with me, and I didn't even notice—

—So you were enjoying the music, so what?

I wanted to believe him but I knew he thought I was a dick really.

—No, I started to say, then someone pushed past us. I looked up and it was Karen and Mackers. Mackers was behind Karen steering her out of the room by her bum.

I looked at Julie and Bonanz. They were snogging.

I looked at Nicola and the scruffy fella. They were snogging as well.

I looked back at the OK fella. We were snogging.

9.

I woke up on one of the mattresses in the living room. I wasn't sure if I was dead or not. There was a tin of beer beside my head and the smell of it was making me want to boke, but it would make me boke quicker if I moved my head. I lay there and tried to figure out what was wrong. Sometimes you have that feeling when you wake up from being pissed, you know something's happened.

I lay there for ages, I didn't want to move cos I knew I'd be sick. I couldn't remember anything much but I felt hot and ashamed. I'd been dancing about and singing and making a dick of myself. I'd made a good start in the squat and now it was ruined.

After a long time I moved a wee bit off the mattress, to tug at Nicola's coat lying on the floor beside me. I shrugged it over my shoulders and concentrated on not dying of headache and shame.

After another bit I caught on there was something else wrong with me, not just the washing machine stomach and the thumping head. I didn't know what it was but then it didn't matter cos I knew, sudden and urgent and fast, that I was going to boke.

It near killed me to get to the bog and I boked for ages, vodka and cider and bits of pizza that made me boke again and again when I smelt it. Then I lay on the cold floor, wanting to die. Then after a long time I went back into the living room and I saw the OK fella lying on the mattress beside mine. Then I knew what was wrong and where the other pain was coming from.

10.

I couldn't lie still I was so scundered and so fretting. But I couldn't get up either. I lay doing what my ma calls tossing and turning, trying to find a cool place on the mattress for my sorry dome. Me and the OK fella had done it. We'd done It. We'd Done It. I wasn't a virgin any more. I'd Had Sex.

It was too much to think about. I'd never felt as bad, not even when Colabottlehead had made me cry in front of everyone. I kept forgetting about it for a wee bit, then I'd remember something else, and the shame would come back, clenching my stomach and making me moan. My heat rash was out I was so scundered. I wanted to move away from the OK fella

James his name was James

but I didn't want him to wake up. I'd've died rather than spoke to him, and I mean it. So I lay there and shivered and the memories kept coming into my brain even though I tried to stop them.

I remembered thinking everyone thought I was a dick, cos I'd been dancing stupid or something. And then there was snogging but I didn't know how it'd started. I think I remember freaking out a bit after the joint

joint, yeah, we had a joint!

and then I remember sitting on the floor with my legs crossed and my head in my hands. I think I cried but I couldn't remember proper, my eyes felt tiny and sore but that could've been the hangover, or maybe Es made your eyes go like that, I didn't know. I remember kissing again, then nothing, then my jeans were being opened but I couldn't remember how come I was on the floor with my T-shirt pushed up and my bra open. It was really uncomfortable, my bra being open like that, cos every time I moved the wire dug into me. But I knew where I was for a second cos I said not to open my jeans, but then I forgot I said that and I sort of forgot where I was as well, and the next thing I remember is someone tugging at my jeans and me lifting my bum up so they'd come off easy. I think I remember thinking Why not? and that it was like a script, already decided, the way I'd thought when I'd seen Julie and Bonanz snogging earlier. I knew it was going to happen, it was like someone had already decided it for me. And I do remember sitting up and grabbing the fella and pulling him down on top of me.

I was so scundered I couldn't move, so when I heard someone come into the room I just lay there. I didn't close my eyes, but. I heard the person come in front of me and whisper my name, but I didn't say anything. I couldn't. Then they got down in front of me and it was Nicola.

I just stared at her, I couldn't speak. Nicola said later I looked like a shot animal.

—C'mon out, she whispered at me. But I couldn't move. She went away and came back with a tin of Coke for me. At first I thought I was going to boke it back up, even sitting up to drink it near killed me, but a couple of minutes later I felt a wee bit better, enough to get up and wobbily follow her out onto our rusty balcony.

She lit up a smoke, and at the smell of it I did boke. But I was outside now so it didn't matter, I just leaned my head over the ladder and let the Coke up. I curled up on the platform after, taking up all the room, cos I couldn't even manage to sit up. I just wanted to lie there and die.

Nicola took a big draw of her smoke. I listened to her. Then she gave a big hiss in of breath and sort of choked. She could've fell off the balcony for all I could've done about it, but after a long bit I sort of realised she was in pain and said from the floor, —What's wrong?

—I don't know, she said, —it hurts—

—Yeah, my head's thumping, I whispered.

—No, not my head, my—

She shut up.

We were going to talk about it, what I'd done. I knew it, I could feel it. *It hurts*, she'd said, and she must mean something about being pregnant, maybe it was kicking. So we'd talk about that, and then it'd remind her to ask me how come the OK fella, James, was lying beside me this morning, and I was too sick to lie to her—

She finished her smoke. Thank god, it was making my head spin. Birds were twittering somewhere. If I'd've had any energy I'd've threw something at them. My head would've been best.

—Did you do it with that fella? Nicola said. Suddenly.

—Yeah—

I couldn't lie, I was too sick.

I was near too sick to wait for what she was going to say. If you'd've told me yesterday I was going to tell Nicola I'd done it with a fella I'd've told you to wise yourself up.

—I did it with that other fella—

I sat up, fast. It took me ages getting my eyes back into focus.

—But what about—

The baby, I was going to say, could you do it when you were pregnant? Nicola got there before me. —It didn't make any difference, she said.

The sun was out now. I lay back down in it and curled up again, quietly like a lizard. Nicola must've been dying as well cos she didn't seem to mind we were only saying one sentence every couple of minutes.

My aches spoke to me again. I said to Nicola,

—Did it hurt?

—Yeah—

Nicola smoked half of another cigarette before she said to me, —Did it hurt for you?

—Yeah. I mean no. I mean—

I can't remember was what I wanted to say, but only ***SLUTS*** didn't remember. —It hurts now, I said.

—So does it for me—

There was another long pause. Then Nicola said,

—Is it meant to hurt, do think? Only it didn't with Gonzo—

So we talked about Gonzo, at last, all the stuff I'd been dying to ask and now I couldn't care less about cos I was curled up on this steel platform wanting to die. I'd been gagging to know what had happened – not the gory bits yuk but just how it'd happened, how people got from snogging to taking their clothes off and having sex. I didn't care about Gonzo any more but I still wanted to know How do you say to someone I want to have sex with you? Does it just happen? How do you talk about condoms, and if you have one how can you tell the fella you do without him thinking you're a ***SLUT***?

I wished I didn't feel so shite.

But I still wanted to know what'd happened between me and the OK fella and I hoped talking to Nicola would give me some clues. So I asked her, —How do you know if the fella wants to? How did you know he wanted to?

—Hah, Nicola said. She said they always want to and it's a full scale war not letting them. (Sometimes not, she said, taking a reddener, and then laughing cos she didn't have to be scundered any more, not now that I'd done it as well.)

She'd said before about going upstairs with fellas at parties – I knew that, they all did, and everyone except me got to do it. Nicola or Paddy or Leanne or whoever it was would come downstairs afterwards, giggling, and going —Bloody *octopus*! Hands everywhere—

She got a bit upset then. It might've just been the hangover, but she's not normally a sad sack, Nicola. Maybe it was her hormones again. She said,

—They try and slip the hand and you say No and they say OK and then they slip the hand again and you say No again, and they say Come on, and you say No, and all you can think is what they're going to tell their mates, and even if you've been having a laugh snogging them you're not any more cos you're just waiting for them to slip the hand again—

I lay curled up on the rustbucket of a platform and let her go on at her own pace. I was dying too much to ask questions.

—Anyway, he tried it on on the Saturday night, in the shed, and then on the Sunday I was a bit blocked and I just thought—

Hang on. My head it hurt but I had to jump in here.

—*Sunday*? I squawked.

She looked scundered again.

—Em, yeah, I went round on Sunday to see if he was all right after getting took home by the peelers, and his ma and da were out, so we nuck some of his da's whiskey and sat up in his room—

—What'd you go round for!

—I told you, to see if he was all right after the peelers lifted us—

You didn't come round to see if I was all right, my head said, very small, through its hangover and then surprised me by making me near cry. I crinkled up my eyes to stop me gurning.

—Anyway, Nicola was saying, —we started snogging and then things just sort of happened—

This didn't help.

—But how did it happen? I croaked.

—I don't know, we were just kissing, and then he took my top off, and I let him, and I let him do, em, other stuff, so then there didn't seem any point saying No—

She looked across the houses.

—He said he wouldn't tell anyone, she said.

I sneaked a look at her. I thought she was about to cry.

—I can't believe we just did it. But we couldn't get the condom on so we just did it anyway, I thought it'd be OK, he said he'd pull out but he didn't—

I sat up fast again. Condom! Had he used one! Was I pregnant!

I didn't think my thoughts could feel any worse, but now I knew they'd only been playing games with me. I could be pregnant! Right now! How could you tell? How soon would you know? What would I do if I was?

I knew I was, already. I just knew it, and they always said women always knew. I'd thought Nicola was talking shite when she said that, but she'd said she just knew, and she was. If I knew I was I must be. It didn't matter it'd only been the first time, Nicola had burst that bubble big time.

My head hammered.

—It didn't hurt though, Nicola said. —Well, not as much as I thought it would've, and I thought it was always meant to the first time—

I didn't say anything.

—It hurt you, didn't it? she said.

—Mmm—

She thought for a bit. —Maybe it's always meant to, and Gonzo did it wrong—

—But what about them women in films and porno? I said, —they love it—

There was another long pause.

—I don't know—

We sat there for a while in the sun, until I came round a bit. Then we got cold, and I could hear people moving in the flat, so we went into town to get something to eat with the last of the money from yesterday. I was like an old woman getting into town, but by the time I had a fry in me I wasn't too bad. But I could hardly talk I was so worried. I went to the bogs in town, the one where we'd met Karen, and there was blood in my knickers. Maybe it was my period, I thought, but then maybe it was just cos it was my first time. I didn't know!

I finally told Nicola. I couldn't help it, I was starting to really freak out.

—You're probably not, she said.

—How do you know?

—We couldn't both be, that'd be mad—

I said, That's the same as saying You can't get pregnant your first time.

Who cared. I was near done with my bottle of Bucky and there was a joint going round and good music on the stereo. I wanted another E but no-one seemed to have any, or they weren't offered anyway.

I'd been going to leave if the OK fella had of been there when we got back, or if he'd told everyone like Gonzo had done on Nicola. But when we'd got in Karen just said We got yis some drink, and it was hard to tell but no-one seemed to be looking at us funny.

I started my Bucky.

Karen shouted,

—Virgins til last night!

She was pointing at me and Nicola.

I near fainted. But she shouted again.

–E virgins! Til last night!

I was so relieved I near wet myself.

—Were you? Mackers said. Just to Nicola, of course.

—Yeah, she said.

—What'd you think? he said.

Again to Nicola, but stuff it, I didn't care. I was still flying a wee bit from last night and I could take on bloody stupid bloody Mackers any time he wanted.

—It was brilliant, I said.

Some fellas came in later, four of them I think, and I wasn't bothered at all. And everyone paired off again, and I paired off too, with a fella called Tommy. I'd done it once now so it didn't matter, so I did it again, only this time I remembered about a condom. But he didn't have any but he said he'd pull out, and this time I remembered doing it and it still hurt. But it didn't the next night.

11.

I was crying in the bog. Not bawling, just standing with my hands against my eyes, going into them *thankyouthankyouthankyou*. There was fanny pads in Karen's bag so I got one then I went in and told Nicola. We screamed and jumped around and laughed, but it was OK, everyone just thought we were wasted.

Karen and Mackers were having a row. It was probably cos we hadn't nuck anything that day. It's easier than you think but it's still hard, nicking stuff, sometimes you just don't get the right chance. She'd nuck an electric razor from Poundstretcher instead, to sell, but Mackers was raging cos he wanted drink now and the fella who bought the stuff off them wasn't in til about six.

I hadn't met this guy yet, cos we'd only been here five days and Karen said he'd be too suss of us yet. But I imagined him, I had visions of some guy working in a suit and office all day, then coming back to the estate and putting on a tracksuit and a balaclava and buying the stuff everyone'd nuck while he was at work.

Anyway.

—Get some money will you! Mackers was shouting. She was telling him to piss off, but she was near crying as well. He was a git. He reminded me of Paul.

Me and Nicola sat on the floor, letting on we weren't listening.

—RIGHT!! Karen screamed.

She got up and ran over to the door, pulling her fleece on her as she went. Mackers got up as well and said, —Wait, I'll come with you—

They slammed the door.

They must've got a sub from the fella's mate for the electric razor, cos they had drink when they got back an hour later, Bucky and cider. Mackers took a bottle of Bucky and a barrack buster and twenty smokes for himself. Me and Karen and Nicola had two barrack busters and twenty smokes between us.

—Did he give you a sub? I said to Karen.

—Yeah, she said

and we got stuck in again.

—WHAT?! Karen shouted.

The music was on loud, so luckily no-one heard her. I'd only asked her if she'd ever thought she was up the duff cos was it OK for fellas to pull out. Nicola was talking to someone else so cos I was drunk I let on I was more drunk than I was and I asked Karen. I didn't like fellas pulling out but they said they wouldn't use condoms cos they couldn't feel anything. And I never really knew if they pulled out or not, cos what did it feel like if they did, or didn't? Do you and Mackers use them, can fellas really not feel anything, was what I really wanted to ask her but I didn't know how.

—Are you not on the pill!

She was near fainting with the shock.

—Em, no, I said.

—What's Nicola use?

I was scundered, scarlet. If Nicola heard she'd kill me.

—I think she's on the pill, I said.

—Well, get her to give you some—

This was thinking on your feet all right. —I think she's only got a couple left—

—For god's sake, Karen said. —How do you think you're going to be able to stay here if you're up the duff?

I didn't know how to defend myself. —But the fellas won't use anything—

—Course they won't, and you can't trust them to pull out either, you have to get the pill—

Sometimes Karen forgot me and Nicola were only culchies. But she saw my face. She said, —I'll get some.

She gave me a wee brown paper bag. I locked myself in the bog. There were six wee foil packs in the bag. MARVLON, the foil said. There were days written on the foil. MON TUE WED THU FRI SAT SUN, they said three times each. There was no leaflet with them.

It was Sunday today I thought, so I took a SUN pill. I was excited now, I wanted to know what it felt like without fellas having to pull out.

Nicola thought she saw Paul. We'd been there a week and a bit, nine days I think. She'd gone to the shop to get hangover stuff, and when she knocked the code on the balcony door to be let back in she near hammered the glass in. Jesus Christ, said Mackers, is she trying to break the bloody door in or what. I let her in and we went into one of the bedrooms and she told me she'd seen Paul, she was sure it was him.

—It was his red coat, and he had the same hat, and the big gorilla arms—

—But what would he be doing in Belfast—

Nicola thought maybe the peelers had copped on we were in Belfast, maybe someone had spotted us on the bus or the bus driver had remembered us or something. We were talking about Kelly on the bus, she said.

We were. We were stupid bitches. But I didn't know why Paul'd be here, even if he did want to act the big man and try and kick ass. He couldn't give that much of a shit.

Nicola said,

—But I betcha the peelers know we're here—

I thought she was right.

I didn't go out the next day. Me and Nicola had went back out round to the shop, and I'd seen the fella in the red jacket and it was Paul. Nicola thought now that it wasn't, but I said I'd know my own stepda. So the peelers must know we're in Belfast, cos they would've told him, and he'd found out somehow where me and Nicola were and he was just waiting to catch us.

—It's not him, Nicola said. But it was, I knew it.

Mackers said I was taking the piss. I hadn't went out the next day but it was the day after that and he said I had to wise up and stop lying about on my arse and expect everyone else to do everything. I had to say something so I said I didn't want to go out cos there was a fella about who looked like someone from home. —Who? he said, and when I said about the red jacket he laughed and said —Sure that's only Jimbo—

I didn't know whether to believe him or not, but he wasn't going to let me stay in the flat all day so I had to go out nicking with Karen and Nicola. We didn't see the fella in the red jacket again so I didn't know who he was, but I still thought Nicola was right, the peelers must know we were in Belfast. And I thought she might be wrong as well cos maybe it had been Paul, and Mackers was talking shite. I hated going out after that, I felt all jumpy and stretched like I was on speed.

One time we saw a young fella in town, sitting beside the bus station crying and letting on he wasn't crying. He had blood all over the back of his head and all over his hands where he was trying to stop the blood. He had a wee rucksack as well, and you could spot he was run away a mile off. —Will we go over and see if he wants to come back to the flat, I said to Karen, but she said, —Nah, he'll be all right.

It was funny I thought cos she'd asked us to come back no bother.

Julie was funny too, she never talked to me and Nicola even though we tried to talk to her. She'd gone into the bedroom with Bonanz the night after me and the OK fella had done it, but she was with another fella the next night, a big gorilla looking thing I never saw at the flat again. (I never saw the OK fella again either, but it wouldn't've bothered me now I'd done it with a couple of other fellas.)

I still didn't really like Julie even though I knew her a wee bit better now. She had this attitude like she thought me and Nicola were dicks. Like one time I said to her she must've been robbing all day to come back with the amount of money she did (near two hundred quid), and she just looked at me like, who is this creature and why is it talking to me? I got all nervous then and said to her —How come you go out on your own when you're getting money anyway, do you not like company? It was only a joke but she gave me a really snattery look and turned away and went and sat down away from me.

We went out one night when we were rich, it was brilliant. We went to a club in the city centre, me and Nicola and Karen all dressed up with loads of makeup and false IDs Mackers got for us. Mackers came as well, but Bonanz and Julie didn't. We drank in the house for a bit but Mackers said not to drink too much or we wouldn't get in. Then we got a taxi into town and took our Es just before we left the house. It was mad trying to climb down the ladder in what we were wearing. We were all in short skirts and high heels, though I'd made sure I had some tights on cos there was no way I was flashing my corned beef thunder thighs in public. Karen had nicked them for me earlier, she'd got them too small but I wore them anyway. Karen and Nicola had just put false tan on, and of course they looked great. —See, Mackers said to me, —there's no need to wear tights—

I wished I hadn't wore them later, cos I had to take them off when I was out the back with a fella, and it was fiddly and difficult drunk in high heels, trying to step out of tights. In the end the fella said he'd give me a hand, and together we ripped them off. I held my knickers in my hand though, there was no way I was losing them as well with the shortness of that skirt.

I don't know who the fella was, I didn't even know his name. I'd saw him talking to Mackers a bit before, looking over to me and Karen and Nicola. There were a couple of other fellas there as well. One of them came over to Karen as soon as I looked over, and when he came over she looked over at Mackers. He nodded at her, probably to say Yeah, go on ahead if you want to. Karen did go out with other fellas even though she was sort of with Mackers. He didn't seem to mind.

Anyway, this fella came over and said —Hi, and I said —Hi back, and he said —Do you want to go outside, and I said —Yeah – cos my E was working now and I felt like it. He was the first fella since starting my pills I think, I think I was nosy to know what it would feel like without him having to pull out. He did it to me over a car, it was cold and I was scared someone would see but he said it would be all right. Afterwards we went back in and he left me at the door and went back over to Mackers and I went back over to Nicola. —Are you all right? I said to her, cos she'd been left there on her own while me and Karen had been out with the fellas. She said she was grand, one of Mackers' mates had been over a minute ago asking her if she wanted to go outside but she'd said No. —How come? I said, thinking she was boring. She said she just didn't feel like it. But the fella had tried to make her, grabbing her arm and saying Come on. Nicola had said No again, and the fella had went back over to Mackers.

—Which one is he? I asked her.

—Him, over there, in the checked shirt—

I saw him. He was talking to Mackers, fast and looking annoyed, and Mackers was talking fast back. After a bit Mackers gave him some money. He must've been buying blow.

Nicola only did it one more time. She said she just didn't see the point of it, cos it hurt and the fella didn't even talk to you after. It was with the fella from the club, the one who'd tried to get her to go outside with him. He was at one of our parties a couple of nights after, and he sat beside Nicola all night. At first she was snattery to him, but he worked hard on her and after a bit she was OK with him. She didn't go into one of the bedrooms with him, cos the rest of us were already in them, but I came into the living room at about five to get a smoke and she was sitting on the floor with the fella on one of the mattresses.

We went out to the balcony for a smoke and she told me she'd done it with him.

—I'm not doing it ever again, she said. —It was really sore and then he just fell asleep and left me lying there like a dick—

—It wasn't sore for me this time, I said.

—Well it was for me—

She moved a bit, then did one of them wee gasps she sometimes did when she climbed up the ladder. She said,

—It's really sore still. It feels like period pains or something—

12.

—I'm bleeding, Nicola said later on that day.

At first I thought she meant it was something to do with the E, she was coughing up blood or puking it or something. But then she looked really scundered and said —From, you know, so I knew, sort of knew, it was something to do with her being pregnant.

—When did it start? I said, trying to sound all professional.

—I don't know, it's been hurting since last night, but I thought it was cos of that fella, but then I went to the toilet and there was blood—

We were in the bathroom after Nicola had come to get me out of the living room. There wasn't a lock on the door, so I sat against it while Nicola sat on the bog and we tried to figure out what was happening. I had my smokes in my pocket, a full twenty deck, so we had one each while we tried to figure out what was going on.

—I was bleeding one time after as well, I said, —maybe it's that—

—But there's a lot of it, were you not just bleeding a wee bit? This is like I'm taking my period, it feels like it in my back as well—

So maybe it was something else. Any kid who watches Holby knows that if someone's up the duff and they bleed that it's probably a miscarriage, but even if we knew that we still didn't know what actually happened during one, or what to do anyway. We couldn't go to hospital cos then we'd get caught and brought back home, and I didn't know about Nicola but I was having a far better time in the flat than I ever had in Craigavon. I couldn't go back even if I was having a shit time, Paul would kill me.

I wished now I'd told Nicola about Paul hitting me, I'd've had plenty of chances to do it since we'd spent most of the last couple of weeks pissed and I could've told her without being too scundered. I don't know why I didn't, it was still too scundering I think even if I was wasted. But she didn't know now, so I'd have to hope her ma and da would be enough to keep her at the flat.

—Do you think you have to go to the hospital? I said to her.

—I dunno—

When you see this on TV it's always a big panic, and *I'm bleeding*! and *Doctah, will I lose the bayby*? but I don't think Nicola was worried about any of that. She hadn't even wanted the baby in the first place, and she still didn't. I don't even think she thought of it as a baby. At least, I was the only other person who knew about it and I never thought of it like that, it was just *Nicola'spregnant!*

I looked up at her to see if I could get a clue from her face. But my look stopped at her jeans cos there was blood seeping out from between her legs. It looked like the world's heaviest period and I could've swore I could even see the blood coming out, the stain spreading bigger like when you drip water on cloth. I panicked a bit, but I looked away fast from the blood cos I didn't want Nicola looking down and seeing it. If it'd been all that blood coming out of me I'd probably have fainted.

I was a bit scared then. It didn't look like she was just bleeding cos of the fella, so maybe she did need to go to the hospital. But I didn't say it, not yet, cos maybe I'd read Nicola wrong and she'd collapse in a dramatic heap on the floor if I said Here, I think you're having a miscarriage. It wasn't too likely I thought, but she might, people on TV always went mental if it was a miscarriage even if they never wanted the baby before.

But of course I wasn't being as noble as I'm letting on here, cos of course I was scared to go home cos of Paul, never mind Colabottlehead and her mates definitely lining us up for a kicking now, or the peelers charging us with the headbutt as well as nicking the Man U shirt. Nicola would be all right even with all that, cos she had her ma and da. Even if she had ran away, they'd be well chuffed to see her turn up at the front door again, they'd kill the fatted calf and everything. Whereas if I turned up at my ma's front door, Paul'd probably take the hinges off it and beat me round the head with it.

I tried to think what to do, but Nicola decided it for us.

—I think, she said, shifting her arse on the toilet seat, —it'll be all right, it's probably just from that fella last night—

But that was when the decision was made for us, cos then Nicola dipped her head down and took a look at her jeans. She let out a funny sort of wee moan and lifted her head up again and looked at me. She'd gone white. She still had her eyeliner on from last night, she looked like a Goth.

—Lisa—

—It's all right—

—Lisa, what is it, what am I going to do?

I hated Gonzo. If he'd been there right in front of me right at that moment I'd've happily ripped his balls off and wore them as ugly hairy earrings. What was he doing now, while Nicola was lying bleeding in this shitty bathroom? He probably hadn't even thought about her being pregnant, he probably hadn't thought about it at all apart from those days after when he was mouthing off to everyone in our class about it and being Mr Bloody Superstud—

Someone laughed in the next room, over the music.

—Lisa, I don't want them knowing—

—Stay here then—

—I can't, I can't stay in here all day, someone'll need in—

Nicola she speaketh the truth. And if she, we, waited til someone wanted into the bog before we went out, they'd see the blood on her jeans—

But if we went out where would we go?

—Do you want to go into one of the rooms? I said.

—No, someone'll come in—

—Do you want to go outside, I said, not knowing how she could, but not knowing what else to say.

—I'll have to, Nicola said.

The lack of sleep, and the E, and the hangover, were all making this very weird. I had this feeling again that everything was already decided, like it was a script.

—OK, I said.

Nicola looked down at her jeans again. I read her mind. Drugs must give you telepathic powers or something, they should tell you that instead of saying you'll end up slumped in a gutter with a needle hanging out of your arm—

—I'll see if I can get you trousers—

We opened the bathroom door and stuck our heads out. It was like being a secret agent or something, only it was shite. Clear coast. We ran down the hall to one of the bedrooms. Or at least I ran, cos when I looked back Nicola was staggering towards me with wee baby steps.

—Does it hurt? I said, thinking as I said it that it was a dimwit question, but Nicola said —No, but my jeans are wet and I can't walk properly—

So I ran into the bedroom and started looking for Nicola's bag. I couldn't find it. It must be in the front room where the rest of them were, and I couldn't really just stroll in, lift it and say Nicola's maybe having a miscarriage so she just wants a change of clothes, all right?

The room was a tip and I didn't have time to look, but I knew already I wasn't going to find the bag, cos it was in the script. I saw a pair of Karen's combats and grabbed them instead. Nicola was still in the hallway, knees bent together like a fat woman in a seaside postcard.

I didn't say anything, just held the combats up and went down the hall. Nicola followed me. I thought the door of the living room was going to open and Julie or Karen or one of them would come out and want to know what was going on and why we were nicking Karen's combats. I thought our luck had been shit up to now and was still being shit so that's what was going to happen. But it didn't. We opened the door and crept down the ladder like two kids sneaking away from trouble.

The alley was stinking. But we couldn't move cos Nicola was really sick now, and she was relying on me to keep her right and I didn't know what to do. It's harder than you think trying to find somewhere to have a miscarriage. Or a heavy period which is still maybe all it was, Nicola had said she was having period pains. Maybe the sex had made her have a period even though she was pregnant? I didn't know!

We'd went to the first place we saw and got her into the combats. It's lucky they were black cos the blood was coming out of her fast now, her jeans and knickers were soaked with it. But just when I went to say to her not to worry, no-one'd see the blood on the combats, so we'd be able to find somewhere better to sit, she was looking at me, scared, big eyes like a frightened kid. —Lisa, she says, then she kind of slid down the wall of the alley on to the ground.

—Nicola the ground's wet, is all I could think of saying, dimwit me cos I don't think Nicola could've give two flying shits about the ground at that minute. She was dead white, you could near see through her skin. —Nicola do you want to go to the hospital, I said, but she didn't answer. Her eyes were still open but I don't think she heard me, and as I watched her her eyes shut.

I didn't panic, funny enough. Maybe cos it was too big. I knelt beside her and said Nicola! a few times, and shook her, but I knew she wasn't going to wake up and that I had to get her to the hospital. I didn't want to leave her lying in the alley on her own but I'd have to, to find a phone box and ring 999. So I left her lying there, in the muck.

My chest was all tight cos I thought something would happen to her on her own, and even though I knew I'd no choice except to leave her it didn't matter, I was still leaving her lying there on her own in the muck.

I found a phone box and I phoned the ambulance. I had Nicola's blood all over my hands from helping her on with the combats, I must've looked like an axe murderer. They asked me where

I was and I couldn't tell them and I couldn't breathe. But they told me to look for a street name, and I did and I told them and then I was OK. Then I put the phone down and went back to the alley and waited in the muck with Nicola for us to be caught.

13.
Once when I was in primary school, this is stupid, but once I broke a ruler when the teacher was out of the room. It said on the ruler it was shatterproof, and I thought that meant you couldn't break it. So I bent it right back, and everyone said —Lisa don't, you'll break it! cos our teacher was real strict and she would've killed us soon as look at us. But I went —Nah, it's OK, and I kept bending it back. I wasn't showing off, well not much, I really did think I couldn't break it cos it said it was shatterproof. But then it snapped in half and everyone gasped and when I went under the desk to pick up the half that'd fell I thought I was going to be sick. I could hardly see the ruler, and everything was in slow motion as I bent down and picked it picked it up, and when I had to sit at my desk and wait for our teacher to get back, knowing all the smug wee shites in our class would tout on me, knowing I was dead, I could hardly have said my own name I was so scared.

14.
—I would've just run, Chrissie said, and when I said —You don't run out on your mates, she said —No, but I would've waited til the ambulance people got there then I would've run—

It might've been better. But I didn't run.

In the alley, I tried to get Nicola to listen to me cos we had to get a story together and right for the ambulance people. —We live round here, all right?

...and we were going into town, and Nicola felt sick, so I phoned an ambulance. End. Of.

—And if they say they want to phone our mas we'll just tell them no, cos they can't force us to give them names—

All well and good in my head and how it had always said I should act if something happened, be like a tough cowboy type and refuse to talk. Only today, the day it would have to happen, I was dying and I couldn't handle being asked loads of questions and maybe shouted at. It was like with Colabottlehead and not being strong enough to fight her as well when me and Nicola fell out. I couldn't do it.

I stopped making up the story and I looked at Nicola to see if she'd took any of it in. She'd got sitting up a wee bit, and I think she knew where she was OK, but that was about it. Her eyes were very bright and the green top she was wearing looked like it was pulling all the colour out of her face.

I didn't care about the story now, I was scared. I started talking to her again, to hide the noise of my heartbeat. She'd be OK, we both would, we just had to play it cool, keep our mouths shut, not let on who we were, the hospital couldn't do anything, they might keep her in for a couple of days if she was really sick but then me and Karen would come and get her, or we'd escape her out if the hospital wouldn't let her go—

Her eyes went clear. And then she said, very distinctly,

—I want to go home, Lisa. I'm sick of this and I want my mum—

I didn't want to think about that so I didn't, and then the ambulance people turned up so I didn't have to. There were two of them and they did it just like TV. They asked me what Nicola's name was and then they knelt down beside her and kept saying it. —Can you tell us what's wrong Nicola, we're just going to lift you onto this stretcher Nicola, you'll be fine Nicola.

It was very weird watching her being lifted on to the stretcher. It was like the script again. And I'd never seen this sort of thing before except on TV so that made it worse. They wheeled the stretcher out of the alley and I followed them. No-one had said to but I thought it'd look suss if I just stood there like I didn't care. They hoisted Nicola up into the ambulance and then they saw me.

—Are you her friend, one of them ses to me.

—Yeah, I said.

—Do you know what happened, she said.

I span the story.

—Do you know what's wrong with her? she said.

I didn't know what way the script was meant to go here so I was stuck. I didn't want to say I think she's having a miscarriage, cos saying it would make it true and I wasn't meant to know about stuff like that anyway, it would make us both sound like ***SLUTS***. So I said instead, —She's bleeding—

They looked at each other over the top of my head, I could feel them. I could feel them getting ready to ask something else as well. Then she said,

—Do you know if Nicola has a boyfriend?

—No, I said.

—No you don't know or No she hasn't?

—No she hasn't, I said.

Well, she didn't.

We weren't long in the ambulance, ten minutes maybe. My teeth wouldn't stop chattering. I looked at Nicola. She had her eyes closed but I think she was awake. She was the same colour as cottage cheese.

And she wanted to go home.

15.

We got caught. Course we did, I'm not writing all this for the good of my health. And I didn't expect anyway that we could just turn up at a hospital and Them not twig how old we were or that we were run away. Chrissie said Nicola was obviously caught cos she couldn't go anywhere and there was nothing I could do about that, but me, if I hadn't of run when the ambulance people got there I should've just slipped out the ambulance door and round the corner when they were taking the stretcher out. She said people in hospitals know to look for dodgy stuff and once I went in the door that would've been it, I'd've been finished cos they'd know rightly. Nicola wouldn't've minded if I'd bailed, Chrissie said, she would've understood.

She might have. I think I would've. She'd be OK now, she was going to the hospital and there was no point the both of us getting scooped. But it's OK for Chrissie to say about slipping out the ambulance door cos of course when they took Nicola out on the stretcher I could hardly run off with them looking at me, I had to go too.

Anyway, one of the ambulance people ses to me to come in and give Nicola's details to the ward sister. Bollocks, I thought, but like I say I couldn't exactly have done a runner with them all looking at me, so I had to follow them into the hospital. I hate hospitals. I think everyone does but I really do. It's the smell of them I think, and the way everything's too clean, and the old people you see sitting about in wheelchairs making you think, I'm going to end up like that. My ma brought me in once when I was ten after she thought Paul'd dislocated my shoulder. He hadn't, but I couldn't move my arm and the neighbour saw me and ses to my ma Maybe you should get her checked out at the hospital, so my ma had to then. She left me sitting outside X-ray on my own and she went out for a smoke and she was away for ages, I thought she'd abandoned me. It happens.

The two ambulance people were swapped for two fellas in blue jumpers and trousers and we went down a corridor and through two big doors and then there was a lift. I looked at Nicola but she had her eyes closed. We got out of the lift and along another corridor and through more doors with the stretcher and then down a ward. I trailed behind like I was going to the electric chair. I thought maybe the fellas in the blue jumpers didn't know I was meant to give the details to the ward sister whatever that was, so maybe I could just sneaky sneaky back, just slide down the corridor a wee bit—

They looked round. I had to let on now of course I wasn't trying to do a runner, which meant I had to smile at them and go up to the counter they were at.

The fellas in the blue jumpers went away. I was left with two nurses, one was in a blue uniform and fat and with massive tits like the matron in the Carry On films and she was about fifty, and the other one was maybe my ma's age and in a white uniform. I don't know why my brain was noticing all this but it was.

I must've looked like a rabbit caught in the headlights as I stood there waiting for one of them to say something. I was sweating. I could smell drink off me and the hospital was too warm and it was making me feel sick.

It was the big one who spoke to me, the scary one. That's the one who's in charge, Chrissie said to me later and I said Sure I know that Chrissie, do think I'm thick? Anyone would know she was in charge by the way she looked and the way she spoke, she was like those huge teachers who used to make you cry in primary school just by shouting at you a wee bit.

She only said, —Now, what's your friend's name, please? but you could tell by the way she said it that she's already decided Something Was Up. It's cos she said please, the alarm bells started ringing. When they say please and go all polite you know they've got you. She might as well have put the thumbscrews on and tied me to a chair.

—Nicola, I said, in case the ambulance people had told the fellas in the blue jumpers and they'd told her. I shouldn't have told the ambulance people her real name but with her bleeding all over the place I couldn't help it, I couldn't think.

—Nicola what—

I couldn't think for a couple of seconds. I'd known really I suppose but I knew now for sure this was it, it was all over. I was too spaced to think of answers in time and to lie properly, and even if I did this woman could sniff out lies like a police drug dog, and even if she didn't Nicola still wouldn't know what lies to back me up on. We didn't know our lines.

She was still waiting for Nicola's last name.

—Hornby, I said.

My knees near dropped from under me when I realised I'd near said Hornball by mistake.

—And her date of birth?

I did like we did with the peelers and I gave Nicola's real birthday but I changed the date to make her eighteen. When the nurse just wrote it down I got a wee flare of hope. Maybe she believed me, maybe they couldn't say anything about phoning mas if they thought Nicola was eighteen—

But then she asked me Nicola's address and my mind died on me, winding down like one of those old records. I couldn't think of any estate names in Belfast. I couldn't think of anything full stop, the E had Judased me.

—Em, I said.

She watched me.

—I can never remember the house number! I said. But I said it too bright and in my dickhead voice and she knew rightly and that was it.

I tried to float even though I knew I was sunk, I said I couldn't remember the name (of the estate where my friend lived, yeah right), but it was just round the corner from where I'd phoned the ambulance. I said she'd just moved and I could never remember the name of her street. I said it was probably in the phone book if they wanted to look it up. I said lots of shite I wouldn't have swallowed myself for a second, telling myself inside my head to shut up shut up can you not shut up you dick, but I couldn't, and all the time the head of the nurse was bent down, writing something on her form and not saying anything, not even letting on to listen to me. I nearly ran then but I didn't. I'd like to say I was waiting for a better time but the truth is I didn't have the balls. (I would've just run out, Chrissie said.) Anyway, I stopped talking cos I'd caught on how squeaky and desperate my voice sounded, but then the silence sounded worse so I started again. Nicola was always sick, she'd fainted in school last week

what school what school they'll ask you, you dick!

and her ma had kept her off—

She cut in. She didn't even wait for me to finish what I was saying cos we both knew it was all a load of shite. I felt like a mouse about to be swallowed by a snake.

—And what's your name? she said.

I said Lisa cos I had to. I didn't know where Nicola was to tell her my name was Kelly. But then she asked my last name and I said, —Em, do you need that? making it even more obvious, but I couldn't help it. —Just for our records, she ses, smiling like that nurse in that Jack Nicholson film set in the mental home, so I said —Rice, Lisa Rice

and I don't know why I bothered.

The next part of getting caught was the big mamma nurse going away but me not able to escape cos of the other nurse still at the counter, then the big mamma nurse coming back with some girl. That was the duty social worker, Chrissie said when I got to this bit, and I said I know that, didn't she tell me? Chrissie thinks she knows everything.

—Lisa? this woman ses to me, and I'm thinking right away that I don't like her. She's got short spiky hair and a nose ring and a clipboard, and she's wearing trainers and big baggy combats like she thinks she's a skater kid or something.

Anyway, I didn't say anything when she said Lisa and then she said what Chrissie said, she was called Liz and she was the duty social worker at the hospital. At the time I didn't know what a duty social worker was, and I didn't really know much about social workers except that a couple of people at school had them and they were always going on about spoofing them and being annoyed by them. She was one of Them anyway, she was just the same as a peeler. Even if she was trying not to look like it with her trendy hair and her skater clothes.

She didn't seem bothered. —Can we go in here, she ses, waving her clipboard over to a room behind the counter.

If the big nurse hadn't of been standing behind me I'd've jumped past them and ran, Nicola or no Nicola. (I would've, Chrissie said. Chrissie was really sickening me.)

Anyway, we went into the room. There was a low table and a row of chairs on one side of the table and another row on the other. This Liz one sat down but I just leaned against the door and folded my arms. —Are you not going to sit down? she said after a bit, but I ignored her. She looked at me for ages then, trying to get me to look at her, but she was going to have a long bloody wait.

She gave up finally. Lisa, she said.

I ignored her. But then she said,

—Lisa, we think you and your friend aren't actually from Belfast—

You'd've thought she was accusing us of being culchies or something, the way she said it. I still didn't say anything but my stomach had turned over and my face went all red and I knew my heat rash was coming out on my neck. (I didn't tell Chrissie any of this bit.)

She put on this gentle, sympathetic type of voice, I think I was meant to make me think she was On My Side (man). She said,

—The thing is, there's two girls missing from Craigavon who are in Belfast, and they're called Lisa and Nicola as well—

How'd you know we were in Belfast, I thought, at the same time as I thought Shit we did speak too loud on the bus. Why had I said Lisa even if Nicola had given her real name, why hadn't I said Kelly?

It's even more like a dream after that. I knew we were caught so I thought I'd just let them do whatever and I'd think about what to do afterwards. That's the best way, Chrissie said, and I near fell off the bed in shock at her agreeing with me for once. Anyway, I sat there while the social worker Liz person went out, and I didn't even try and sneak out cos I knew even without looking that the Big Mamma Nurse was at her wee counter outside the door and that the social worker would've told her to keep an eye on me in case I did a runner.

The police turned up then, and that's how I knew for sure the social worker was really one of Them no matter how she tried to act she wasn't. She came in and gave me this smile, and I wasn't going to smile back even before I saw the peelers behind her. It was two girl peelers, maybe they thought that would be better for me, I don't know. Anyway, I've kind of always wanted to be being asked stuff by peelers and to sit there like someone in a film thinking You'll get nothing out of me coppa. So that's what I did.

They weren't like cops in a film, but. For some reason they were trying to be nice even though it looked like it was near choking them to do it. They said they were just trying to help and nothing would happen if I just talked to them. But I didn't. Then one of them started to act all annoyed, it was like good cop bad cop, it was pathetic. I just sat there and let them do it. I was scared but it was kind of funny in a way, watching them get all wound up. Karen would've been proud of me.

When they both got annoyed they started saying things like —Come on now Lisa! and —You could be in a lot of trouble young lady, don't make it any worse for yourself. Then Bad Cop got really annoyed and said —Come on now, I haven't got all day to waste on you! But the social worker woman gave her a dirty look so she shut up.

—That's all you have to do, Chrissie said, just sit there and say nothing and wait til they give up on you. She's right, it is.

Then Chrissie said, —So what did they say when they caught on you weren't going to say anything?

And that's when they played their Trump Card, cos they said they were going to phone my ma and tell her I'd been found, then they were going to take me home.

I think it showed in my face a bit but I hope it didn't. My stomach squirted panic though. And when I think of my ma and Paul I nearly always think of Nicola's ma and da, cos they're nice and cos it's not fair, so I started thinking about Nicola's ma being told she'd been found as well. Her and Nicola's da'd be straight up to the hospital, and there'd be tears and apologies and lots of Why didn't you tell us. They wouldn't've been over the moon at Nicola being up the duff, course they wouldn't, but I knew they'd be so glad to have her back that it wouldn't even matter that much, they'd just tell her to wise herself up in future. And no-one else knew about it, so when Nicola got out of hospital everything would be the same as always, cept she'd spend a few days getting spoilt first, lying on the sofa watching MTV while her ma and da tried to get her into another school.

I knew already I was going back to the squat as soon as I could get away. And the peelers didn't know about the squat. They kept trying to find out about it, saying things like —Lisa where were you sleeping? and —How did you get the money for food? but I didn't tell them, course I didn't.

16.

The next part of getting caught was, the peelers went out then to phone my ma. Me and the social worker sat there. She seemed to have finally copped on that I wasn't going to say anything, so she just sat there in her baggy combats. I was dying for a smoke but I knew there was no way I'd get out to have one. The peelers were away for ages. Then when they came back they didn't come into the room, they just opened the door, and when the social worker looked up they nodded at her to make her come out into the hall. I sat there. They were away for ages as well. I tried to hear what they were saying, cos they were just outside the room, but I couldn't make them out.

Then they came back in. They had big tragic expressions on their mugs so I knew something was coming. The social worker woman sat on the edge of the low table. I thought for a minute she was going to sit cross-legged on it, just to show me how cool she was, but she didn't. I could see the peelers standing round the door. What the hell was coming now. Maybe they'd found out about the squat and they were coming to arrest me for swiping money and munching Es—

—Lisa, the social worker ses.

I didn't look up, but she knew I wasn't going to so she just went on ahead anyway.

—Lisa, she ses, —I'm afraid your mum has said she doesn't want you back in the house—

17.

I near jumped up and started shouting What! Are you bloody serious! Whoopee freaking doo! cos it was great, it meant I'd escaped for ever. But I didn't want them to think I was a freak or that I cared one way or the other, so I didn't do anything. I looked up in the end, but, cos they were all staring at me. They looked all tragic, like this was a big disaster, but of course it bloody wasn't, it was the best thing that'd ever happened to me as far as I was concerned, apart from finding the squat and passing my nicking GCSEs. They'd have to let me go, I could go back to the squat and get blocked and tell everyone about my Brush With The Law. Sweet!

But then the social worker ses,

—So we're going to have to find you somewhere to stay—

I started talking then, you better believe it. I told them I was all right, I could look after myself, I was mature for my age, I didn't want to go and stay with people I didn't know. I told them to wise up and it was none of their bloody business anyway. The social worker pretended she hadn't heard me, and she went, in that gentle, fake voice —But I'm afraid it is, Lisa—

I wanted to deck her. She hadn't a clue. She thought just cos I'm fourteen that I can't look after myself, when I'd been doing it fine for the last two weeks. They never believe you, Chrissie said. When you say you're doing fine they think you're making it up. They go on about independent living and taking responsibility for your own decisions but they're talking shite.

18.

A temporary care order they called it. The social worker explained it all to me and I let on I wasn't listening but you bet your life I was. They had to apply to someone, a judge or something, to let me have social workers responsible for me, and til then they had this temporary thing that meant they were responsible for me til they applied. —Don't worry Lisa, you'll be all right, the social worker said, cos right enough, I should've been all upset at my ma saying I was never to darken her door again. I thought about that for a bit, and I tried to feel all hard done by, but I couldn't. I was just glad not to be going back to her and Paul and the devil children. Still, though. She was a bitch.

Anyway, there was loads of arranging for this care order thing, and the social worker kept dialling numbers on her mobile then going outside the room to talk, but there was no chance of running, cos she was just outside and cos I knew Big Mamma Nurse would be about as well, and the girl cops were around somewhere too I thought. I'd already decided though to just go along with things for now then run the first chance I got. I was still a bit too spaced to get really worried or think about it too much but I did start wondering where they were going to put me.

The social worker came back in, all smiles.

—Right, that's you sorted! she said, like she was giving me drugs or something and I wish she was, —you're staying for a couple of nights with Mandy and Marty Fay—

Holy shit, they sounded like people from a mad cult. They'd probably try and murder me in my bed, or else sell me for sex to weird old men. I'd escape soon though, so it didn't matter—

—They're really lovely, those two, the social worker was saying, —they've been in this situation loads of times—

Bully for them I thought. Just as long as they didn't cop on to put bars on the windows and security locks on the doors.

19.

I fell asleep in the car, I was raging at myself. I didn't have a clue how long we'd been driving, or how far away from Belfast we were or even whereabouts we were, and I didn't want to ask either. We were in the sticks, I knew that much when I woke up, cos it was pitch black with no street lights and now we'd turned up a wee road and I could hear gravel crunching under the wheels of the car. I tried to let on to myself that we weren't slowing down, cos I didn't want to get out of the car. But when I was still telling myself it the car stopped in front of a big house stood on its own, and the Liz one went, —OK then, here we are! For a second I thought of diving across the seat and nicking the car, cos she'd left her car keys in the ignition, but driving was another thing I didn't know and that Karen was going to have to teach me when I got back.

I got out fast so she wouldn't think I was scared. I arranged my face into not caring. But I had to do it quick, cos suddenly the front door of the house opened. I don't know what freaked me out more, all the bright light suddenly spilling out onto my face, or the two people coming towards me smiling like maniacs and waving their arms about.

—Lisa! the woman one shouts.

—Hi Lisa, the bloke one ses—

OK, now I was scared (I didn't let that on to Chrissie either). I mean, I didn't really think these people were from a mad cult or anything like that, but I didn't know them, and I was meant to stay with them, and I didn't know what was going on, and everyone was looking at me and I didn't know what I was meant to do and all of a sudden I just really missed Nicola and I felt really on my own.

I looked at them instead. The woman one, Mandy, was fat, with long ginger hair, but nice ginger, auburn, and she was tall as well. She was wearing black trousers and a long red top and she had bare feet. The bloke one, Marty, was a bit smaller and he had a beard and glasses. He was wearing jeans and a black T-shirt with the name of some band on it, I can't remember now cos I didn't know the band. He had bare feet as well.

We stood there. I remember thinking it was like a film someone'd pressed Pause on, cos none of us moved and cos the woman's arms had stopped in mid-wave. Then the Liz one coughed a wee bit, and said all bright, —Right then! and the fella gave a wee jump and said —OK, come on in, you two—

The spaced feeling was wearing off cos I was getting more scared, but I still felt like I was in a dream or like I was stoned. I hung back to let them go on ahead of me, and the Liz one turned round and gave me a big toothy encouraging smile. Then she put her hand on my arm and patted it a bit, and I near snarled at her. She did that again she was going to lose her bloody hand—

I went in. There was no hall, just a big kitchen and dining room all in one with a scrubbed wooden table in the middle of it. My ma would've cracked up if she'd seen it cos there was a coffee cup sitting on it without a coaster, and there was some old dinner stuck to it as well, I could see it even from the door. There was a fire, a proper one, and there were yellow walls and lots of bookshelves and a computer. It was different than my ma's house, than Nicola's house even. It was bigger and it had a computer but there was something else as well.

I stood there like a dick, not knowing what to do. Then the Mandy one shouted —Right! to me, scaring the life out of me and making me think No seriously is there something actually wrong with her.

Then she goes,

—First things first, Lisa! Do you want something to eat, we kept some dinner for you—

I didn't want to say Yeah, but I was starving. The social worker had bought me chips from the hospital canteen but I hadn't ate them, cos it would've been like talking to her. It was the same here, but I was starving.

—Em, OK, I said.

—Are you vegetarian? this woman ses to me.

—Em, no—

Vegetarian! I've never been asked that in my puff. Love to have seen my ma's face if I said to her I didn't want the mince for dinner!

—Beef stew then? the Mandy one shouted. I started to think maybe she's deaf. Or mad, cos she started going on to me about the beef stew not being as nice as it usually is cos they forgot to put the stock cube in it, but it's still nice, at least they hope I'll think so, and once I eat it I can go on up to bed if I want but if not they'll be watching TV and I'm more than welcome, or there's an Xbox and DVDs if I'd rather, or maybe I'd like to check my emails or surf a wee bit?

—Em—

What I wanted to do was run out of that house and go back to Belfast and get blocked with Karen, but all I said was the beef stew would be OK.

Then this Marty fella goes,

—I'll get it, you three go and sort things out—

and I near fell over. I've never seen Paul in the kitchen, ever, cept to get a beer. I wish I was joking but I'm not. And here was this Marty one, ladling out stew, and putting it in a saucepan, and putting on an apron, then starting to do the dishes! I started to think I'd maybe led a bit of a sheltered life.

—Have a seat, Lisa! this Mandy one roars at me. Her and the social worker sat down at the table, so I sat down too. The social worker, Liz, she got loads of bits of paper out of her wee leather case thing, and her and Mandy started going through them. I just sat there and watched Marty, cleaning away in his wee apron with not a bother on him. He stopped every so often and wiped his soapy hands on a tea towel (no harm to him but my ma would've had a fit if she could've seen that tea towel), then he'd go over to the cooker and stir the stew a bit and then go back to the dishes. It was great watching him. Even in the squat the fellas had never done anything, it was always Julie and Karen who tidied up, and then me and Nicola as well.

When he started putting the stew into a bowl I stopped looking at him cos I didn't want him to see me or think I was interested. I could feel him coming over to me so I looked at the table. He put the stew and a spoon in front of me. —Be careful there Lisa, it's very hot, he ses, and I near fell over again cos no-one'd ever said that to me in my whole puff either.

Didn't mean I liked him though.

I still felt spaced. I ate the stew and I felt like I was in a dream and I didn't look up from the bowl.

The social worker said, —Right then, I think that's us—

and she got up. She was just going to leave me here, with people I didn't know and who didn't know me. I didn't even know whereabouts I was—

I looked at the clock and it was half ten. It was only about eight hours after Nicola had told me she was bleeding. Eight hours just, and here I was with a different life and probably no-one knew where I was.

I felt tears coming. I looked at the stew bowl really hard and I bit my lip hard til they went away. It was OK cos the social worker was going and the two people I was being left with were seeing her out. When they came back the tears were away.

—How's the stew? the Mandy woman ses, and I didn't answer her but I don't think she even cared.

She showed me my room next. It was up two flights of stairs and past lots of doors but I didn't even look at them, cos I couldn't have cared less. And I couldn't have looked at anything anyway with this woman rabbitting on and on, saying she didn't want me to think I had to go to bed, she was just showing me where my room was so I could go up and sleep whenever I wanted to blah blah blah. She was mad, she never shut up.

I liked the room, but. I didn't let on but it was cool. It was in the attic and it was massive, a big double bed and a TV and DVD player and a stereo as well. There was a door off it and I thought it was a wardrobe but Mandy opened it and it was a wee bathroom just for me. I near cried when I saw it, I hadn't had hot water in ages.

She still waffled on, going on about there's loads of hot water and plenty of clean towels, and clean jammies and nighties in the chest of drawers – and it all got too much. It felt like I was being shown round a hotel or something. I was here, in a house I didn't know with people I didn't know, and I had to just stay here and wait and see what happened, I had no control over it, over my own life. I felt the way you do when you smoke too much blow and you're going to get a whitey – everything coming at you at once and that you think you're going to boke, or faint.

But she copped on. I don't know how she did when she was wittering so much, but she looked at my face and then she shut up. Finally. I could near hear my ears ringing.

If I had to go downstairs and listen to her I was going to crack up. I still didn't want to talk to her but I wanted her to go away. So I said, —I think I'll have a bath and go to bed—

and she left and closed the door behind her and thank god thank god I was on my own at last.

I don't know what was better, the bath, the smoke I had as soon as Mandy was away, or finally having some peace. But oh the bath was beautiful. I didn't even know how sore and tired I was til I got into it and my muscles started shouting What have you been doing to us. I lay in it for ages. I hardly ever have baths cos my ma moans about the hot water (just to be a bitch, she has baths all the time), or else Paul or the devil children bang on the door and say they want in. But this one was great. I used loads of bubble bath, and I washed my hair and shaved my legs, and when I got out I felt loads better.

But then I went over to the chest of drawers in the bedroom to see if I could find something to put on, and there were loads of nighties and pairs of pyjamas all lined up in the drawers. So I started thinking, Who else has wore these? and then I started thinking about all the other people who'd stayed here. I don't mean I thought the nighties and jammies were dirty, I mean it made me think I was just one in a line, loads of people had stayed here and I was the same as all of them. Mandy and Marty were foster parents. And that meant I was a foster child, like Karen.

I stood there for ages with a nightie in my hand thinking about it. Then I got into bed to think about it. The sheets were clean and warm, far better than the smelly coats and blankets from the squat. But I wasn't going to be able to sleep even though I was knackered. I lay and looked at the ceiling and I still felt like I was in a dream. This morning I'd woke up in the squat, with Nicola, and I was one half of Us. We were meant to be drinking tonight. Nicola was pregnant but we weren't bothered cos we had no mas and das to worry about. But now I was in someone else's bed and I didn't know what was going to happen to me. I wouldn't even have minded that so much if I just had of had someone with me, Nicola or Karen or even Julie.

Or even if someone knew where I was.

I'd started crying without realising it. Tears went down the side of my face into my ears, then I turned over and started crying properly, big proper sobs cos I couldn't help it. Even if I got back to the squat Nicola would be back home. No-one knew where I was and I was on my own.

Part III
Me

1.

That morning I knew where I was right away when I woke up. But it still felt like a dream. The day came in from the skylight, and I could hear a rooster so I knew I was in the sticks all right. And it was quiet apart from that, there was no traffic outside or people shouting and laughing or music playing like in the squat. I was somewhere I didn't know and I was still on my own.

It seemed like it was really early, but I don't have a watch so I didn't know what time it was apart from that. I couldn't get back to sleep. I did try but my head wouldn't let me. So I lay on my back and looked up at the ceiling instead. For hours I think. I could hear them moving around downstairs, but I was too scared to go down so I lay there all still.

Someone was coming up the stairs. I turned over fast and lay on my side and let on I was sleeping.

Whoever it was stopped outside the door.

They said,

—Lisa?

It was a woman's voice so it was Mandy. I just lay there. I didn't want to answer her cos then she'd know that I was lying here awake and that I was scared. But she just acted like she knew anyway. She said,

—There's some breakfast downstairs for you, just come down when you're ready—

Feet went away from the door. I could hear them going down the wooden stairs. I didn't want to lie here all day, and I was hungry, but I didn't want to go down all the more now, cos she'd think it was cos she'd said to. I hated her. I turned on my back again and looked at the ceiling again. If I actually had of been asleep when she'd came up I wouldn't've heard her, so I didn't have to go down.

Feet were on the stairs again. I jumped out of the bed and grabbed my clothes. I don't know why I did it, Paul must've got me scared of everything. I pulled on my jeans and got the jumper over my head and pulled it down to my waist while I was getting over to the door.

When I opened it Mandy was standing at the end of the landing. She was out of breath so she must've just got up the stairs.

—Oh, you're up! she ses, sounding all guilty. I didn't answer her but of course she wasn't bothered. She just did a big smile at me and then she went down the stairs so I had to follow her.

My feet felt naked without my boots on. And they were cold cos I hadn't put my socks on. I went down the stairs and into the kitchen with the cold stone floor. Marty was sitting at the table reading a big paper. He didn't see me so I just stood in the doorway cos the madwoman was nowhere about. But then she came out of a door behind me, making me jump and then making me feel like a dick for just standing there in a doorway. She said, —What do you want for breakfast—

So then Marty heard her, so he folded up his paper and looked at me and said, —Well, sleepyhead! I didn't know if he was taking the piss or not. He might be, they must have known I was lying awake for ages. They must think I was a total dick. I shouldn't have cared but I did even though I hated them.

—Just toast, I said, cos I had to say something, cos the madwoman was still looking at me.

—Eggs? Bacon? Or I could do you a fry if you want—

I'd've loved a fry but I wasn't going to say. I didn't answer her about the eggs or bacon either, and there was a big awkward silent moment while Or I could do you a fry if you want floated round the room. But then Marty said, —Come on and sit down Lisa, and he didn't sound bothered at all.

I tucked one of my cold feet under me and looked round at the table. There was a plastic container with cornflakes in it, and a big jug of orange juice. I wanted some but I wasn't going to ask, and there wasn't a glass on the table, so I couldn't help myself. But then Mandy leaned over the table and put down a glass and a bowl and a spoon in front of me. —Help yourself Lisa! she yelled near right in my ear, and by the time I'd recovered from that there was milk and sugar in front of me as well.

So I took some cornflakes. It was something to do and I was hungry. But then I saw something moving out of the side of my eye, and when I looked round there was a big boxer dog bouncing right at me.

I didn't mind cos I love dogs, but Mandy and Marty freaked out. They started shouting at the dog to get away from me. The dog was looking all upset cos they were shouting at it, so I said to them, —It's OK, cos there's nothing worse than a dog looking like it's about to cry, it kills you. I put my arms around the dog and it put its paws up on my knees and gave me a big slobbery kiss.

I hugged it, hard. I was totally scundered when I copped on that for some reason I was about to cry. So I hugged it again to hide my face and then in a couple of seconds I was OK. Still! Near gurning for nothing, and in front of these people! I'd be scundered for ever.

They hadn't noticed. They were all pleased I liked the dog. —That's Molly, Marty said. He said it was lucky cos she'd been sleeping last night when I got here, cos otherwise she would've jumped all over me. She was jumping all over me now, and I didn't mind but he took her outside cos he said I wouldn't get any peace to eat my breakfast otherwise. But I was glad she was there. I liked her.

After I finished the cornflakes I wanted more orange juice cos I still felt a bit spaced and hungover, but Marty'd had some too so the jug was too far now for me to get. I sat there for ages and then I finally said, —Can I have some more orange juice.

I don't know why it was a big deal for me to say, but it was.

Marty looked all shocked.

—Of course you can Lisa, just help yourself—

—Just treat the place as your own, earywigging Mandy shouted over from beside the cooker, —make yourself at home—

Was this home now and how long would I be staying, I wanted to ask. But I was scared they'd say For the duration. And I didn't want to live here.

They were better than my ma or Paul, but they were still scary, and still near the same as social workers.

She made me eggs even though I hadn't said I wanted them. Not boiled with soldiers, so at least she didn't think I was a kid, but scrambled with cheese in them. I wasn't going to eat them but then I did. They were nice, I tried not to let on. There were four bits of toast too, hot and with proper butter on them. I didn't know how hungry I was til I took a bite of that toast, I could've ate it all day.

When she'd seen I'd finished she sat down beside me.

—I thought, she said, —we could go into town and maybe get some clothes for you, what do you think?

What I thought was I'd be back at the flat soon enough so it wouldn't matter, me not having clothes here. And I didn't want new clothes from these people anyway. But I couldn't tell them that, so I said, —I don't have any money—

I didn't want it to sound like I was apologising for it either, so I kind of snarled it a bit.

They looked at each other over my head, I could feel them do it. There was a bit of a pause. Mandy said,

—It's OK, we have some—

Now I was just scundered. I didn't want people to buy clothes for me like I was a kid. I didn't know what to say, but, so I just sat there.

Marty said,

—Lisa, it's all right. We get money from the government to look after you and buy you things you need. It's our job—

I thought of something. I said, —What about my mum and Paul, will they have to pay it back—

I had my head down looking at my plate but I know they looked at each other again over the top of my head, I could feel it.

They must've thought I was worried about my ma and Paul getting the bill, cos when Mandy spoke her voice had gone all gentle, like the social worker's.

—No, she said, —this is on us—

Damn. It would've been brilliant if Paul had got stuck with the bill, it would've really sickened him and it would've served them right.

I really didn't want to go into town, but. I just wanted to be on my own for a bit before thinking about the great escape, maybe watch a DVD or just lie and veg, just not have to be with people and have to talk to them. But I didn't know how to get out of it. I could hardly say I was tired after lying in all morning, and if I said I didn't feel well there'd be a big fuss and I'd never get any peace. So I went. Marty didn't come with us cos he said Molly went mad and destroyed the place if she was left on her own for too long. She'd ate the computer leads last time and they'd had to get new ones. I let on I didn't care but I was interested. Did the two of them never leave the house together? What did they do if they both had to go out, like to a wedding or something? Maybe Molly was OK for an hour or so, and it was only after that that she went all bonkers? Maybe they got her minded? Or maybe Marty just didn't want to go into town so he was making it up—

I didn't ask.

Anyway, so me and Mandy went round the town and looked for stuff for me. I tried not to let it show, but it was better than I thought, it was actually not too bad of a day. I didn't really talk much but Mandy didn't care, I don't think she even noticed, cos she was wittering on so much herself. And we got loads of stuff for me. I thought maybe we were going to get a few pairs of knickers or something, or some socks, and we'd go into Primark and get all the cheap stuff. But we went round loads of shops, and I got to pick my own stuff. I'd wanted proper jeans for ages, instead of the shit stretchy ones Nicola had given me in her house ages ago and that looked like they'd last been worn in the 80s, and Mandy said if I found a pair I liked I could have them in different colours. We went into a jeans shop and I was depressed at first cos I had to get a size 14 and I'd been hoping I was a 12, but then I tried on a class pair of dark blue bootcut ones, and for the first time in my life something fit me the first time. They didn't even look too bad either. My bum was still the size of France, I knew it was, but it didn't look as big in these jeans compared to the stretchy ones.

Mandy laughed when she saw me checking my arse in the mirror, even though I was trying to do it so she didn't know what I was looking at. But she wasn't laughing at me, it was an OK laugh. —I do that too, she ses.

I was so chuffed that my arse didn't look as massive in these jeans that I smiled back at her a bit. I said, —I hate them old jeans.

So she bought me them, and a pair in black and a pair in ordinary blue, and then we got some jumpers. I went over to the fellas' section for them but Mandy said she'd seen some nice ones at the back of the girls' section, so we went over there. No way are them jumpers going to fit me, I wanted to say to her, but I was too scundered to say I felt too fat for them so I had to go into the changing rooms to try one of them on.

It looked terrible. It didn't even cover my arse, and cos I was wearing the crap 80s jeans again I looked as ginormous as usual. Mandy'd told me to come out and show her the jumper on me but I didn't, I was so fat and scundered that I just put on my baggy jumper again and went out.

—Did you not like it, Mandy said, and I went, —No, even though she probably knew rightly it was cos I was too fat for it.

—Try this one, she goes, holding out a blue one, and I was near crying by now so I just took it off her and went back into the changing rooms.

—Try your new jeans with it, I could hear her shouting after me, and I thought Yeah right. But the jumper did look a bit bigger, so I tried it on, and it did cover my arse a wee bit, so I tried the dark blue jeans on with it, and it looked OK. Not great, cos I was still fat and no matter what I wore I wouldn't look great, but definitely something I could wear. I went back out.

—It's OK, I admitted to Mandy. So she bought it for me, and one in burgundy and one in grey, and then a class black wool one that was thirty quid and the nicest thing I'd ever had on me. I near dared to start thinking I might not always look so much like a fat lump.

Then she said did I want some trainers, but I didn't after the dear black jumper, and anyway I don't like trainers and I was happy with my boots. So she said that meant we could spend a bit more on a coat. I got a knee length black one, kind of like leather but not. It was my first new coat, and once we were outside the shop I took the label off so I could take off my ma's rubbish jacket and wear this instead. Mandy made me put the jacket in the carrier bag but I was going to stick it in the bin as soon as we got home.

We went into Boots as well, and I got loads of stuff. Like loads. Shower gel, and shampoo and conditioner, and body lotion and mousse and toothpaste and even makeup cos she asked me did I want some and I thought Stuff it and said Aye. She picked me a foundation and we got brown eyeshadow cos she said it would be good for my eye colour, and blusher cos I was pale (but she didn't say it in a bad way, she said it like she was jealous a bit), and coloured lip gloss. For kissing, she said, and I was scundered. She bought me a toilet bag and a towel as well, and then when we were in the queue she said, —Hang on a minute, and when she came back she had a big bubblebath set tied with a ribbon that she said was a present and just for fun. I was getting paranoid she thought I must be smelly and ugly, but I sort of knew she was just being nice. And I wouldn't even have cared by now if she was only buying all this stuff cos she thought I was too ugly without it. I don't want to sound like Wee Orphan Annie or anything, but I honestly don't think I'd ever had a new thing bought just for me in my life.

When we got home I tried everything on upstairs. The dark blue jeans and the black jumper looked class with the coat, and I didn't even look too fat even though I still looked ugly and with rank hair, even with the makeup. I wish she could've bought me a new face.

I didn't mind too much going downstairs at dinner time cos I felt class in the new jeans and jumper. Molly jumped all over me and got hairs all over the jumper, but I didn't care. Mandy said I looked great, and even though I knew she was only saying it I was happy all the same, it was nice of her.

We had lasagne and salad and garlic bread. It was the first time I'd ever had lasagne, cos Paul shouts if he doesn't get his spuds every day. It was lovely. —Fattening, Mandy ses, patting her stomach and pulling a big gurny face. —So what, Marty ses.

We watched TV after. I was still dead shy of the two of them still, like when you smoke blow with people you don't know, but it was better than last night. There was good TV on as well, they had Sky+.

I thought about Nicola loads, but. I wanted to ask Mandy if she knew anything about her or if she was OK, but I couldn't get the nerve up. Maybe me and

Nicola weren't allowed to contact each other, I'd seen a film once where that'd happened. The two girls in it were in jail for battering an old lady to death like, but still. Maybe once you were In Care

!

they didn't let you contact anyone from before—

I thought about phoning Nicola's house but I couldn't. Nicola's ma and da would probably crack up at me for running away with Nicola, they'd probably thought it was my idea, and if Nicola'd told them anything about what we'd been doing at the flat they'd never want me near her again.

So I went up to bed still on my own and still not knowing where I was and what was going to happen from here.

2.

The next day was Sunday and it was boring. There was still no hope of escaping cos there was no buses, and the only other thing probably was hitchhiking a lift on a tractor. So after I'd had my breakfast I let on I wanted to take Molly for a walk, so I could have a nosy round about the place and see where the main roads and the bus stops were.

Mandy was all delighted I wanted to take Molly out. She got the lead and got it on Molly, all smiles. Maybe she wanted her and Marty to be on their own so they could have a shag. I felt a bit like I was getting rid of even though I knew that was daft cos I was the one who said I'd go out.

But it was brilliant with Molly. Even though she near pulled the arm off me, and everyone we passed went all, —She's taking you for a walk by the looks of things! and I had to laugh back and go —I know!, it was still brilliant. Then I took her off the lead and we went over loads of fields and got all mucky. Molly had a great time, maybe she wasn't allowed to get mucky if Mandy or Marty took her out.

Mandy, Marty and Molly, I realised for the first time. There was definitely something wrong with these people.

I found the main road and the bus stop about ten minutes from the house, and I stood beside it with Molly and had a smoke and thought about my Plan of Action. I could come down here tomorrow morning and try to hitchhike. But the road was pretty quiet so I didn't know how long it would take to get a lift. OK, it might just be quiet cos it was Sunday and we were in the sticks, but still, maybe I shouldn't risk it—

Bus, then. I could sneak out early and get the first bus, early enough so that Mandy and Marty wouldn't even be up. I needed the fare, but there must be some money lying around the house somewhere—

But the first bus would be after Mandy and Marty got up, I knew it would be. It'd probably be around seven or eight, and they were healthy organic types and they had a mad dog, so they'd be up before that. So I had to get out without them seeing me, and get onto the bus before they twigged I'd done a runner. And I couldn't stand on the road waiting for the bus either. We were really out in the sticks here, so there was probably only a bus every hour or so, and I could hardly stand at the bus stop in full view all that time.

Maybe I could say I was taking Molly out again, and then I'd have a bit more time—

But then I'd have to leave her tied to the bus stop to be found, and I couldn't, I'd gurn. Dogs always make you feel really guilty. (And Molly was brilliant at it, I'd kept giving her bits of lasagne the night before til Mandy told me not to be fooled, she'd just had a big feed ten minutes ago. But if you were looking at her big sad wrinkly face you'd've thought she hadn't been fed for a week.)

So. I'd have to know what times the buses were at, so then I could sneak out of the house about fifteen minutes before, and I'd just have to hope they didn't catch on and come looking for me before I got on it.

There was a timetable but it looked ancient. Ithad the name of the stop though, so maybe I could phone Translink later if Mandy and Marty weren't about. Maybe there'd be an early bus, and maybe I could get out of the house before they even woke up, even if they were healthy organic types.

Too many maybes. But there was nothing else I could do.

Me and Molly headed back. I came into the house talking to her all loud just in case they were shagging. But it was OK, they were in the living room with the papers. Mandy was watching Eastenders she'd Sky+'d over the week so I watched it with her, I hadn't seen it in ages. We talked a bit cos I had to ask her who people were and what was going on. Ian Beale had gone mental but apart from that it was mostly the same.

After Eastenders I wanted to plan my escape and pack my stuff ready for first thing in the morning. I'd no bag, so I let on I wanted a drink of water and went into the kitchen and found the carrier bags. I took two big ones and put them up my jumper. Molly was really interested in the rustling, but she was hyper anyway so her sniffing my jumper didn't look too suss.

I couldn't think of an excuse for why I was going upstairs, so I just went up anyway. But no-one said anything. I put my new stuff in the carrier bags. I felt a bit shite cos Mandy had just bought me all this stuff and here I was clearing off with it, so I thought maybe I should leave one of the pairs of jeans but in the end I didn't.

When I went back downstairs they were looking all serious. My stomach dropped on me cos I thought they'd copped on to what I'd been doing. But then Mandy said,

—Liz phoned—

Nicola was all right. They didn't know if she was still in hospital or at home, cos Liz'd been speaking to the nurse first thing this morning (so Mandy said Liz said anyway).

But.

I was being moved cos I wasn't from Belfast so it was a different office who had to deal with me than who Liz and Mandy and Marty were with. Mandy said Liz had found me a place in a 'unit'. She said it all bright, like Liz had done great and like

I should be delighted. A unit! What the hell was that? It sounded like a jail.

—So you'll be going first thing tomorrow, Mandy ses.

Ha, I thought, that's what you think—

So I'd have to sneak out of the house before first thing tomorrow. But I didn't get the chance to phone Translink, cos Mandy and Marty (and Molly) were in the living room with the phone the whole night. So I still didn't know what times the buses were, and if I left really early like I'd have to I might have to wait for ages. I'd have to maybe leave and hide somewhere til later on, maybe I could hide somewhere where I could keep an eye on the road and run down if I saw a bus—

I'd figure something out. The main thing was to get away.

I went up to bed early, letting on I was tired. But I couldn't sleep. I lay awake for hours shitting myself about tomorrow.

3.

I'd be a shit spy. I wasn't too bad a criminal, but I still wouldn't fancy my chances escaping if I got caught. It was Mandy and Marty's fault. They did get up dead early, and they snuck around all quiet so they didn't wake me. So I slept in.

I couldn't help it. I didn't get to sleep for ages cos I was so hyper and nervous, and then when I did I was so knackered I conked out and slept til half nine on the kitchen clock. That's early enough for me if I don't have to go to school, but not early enough when you're planning to do a runner back to Belfast.

I couldn't believe it when I woke up. I felt sick. I wouldn't even have woke up in the first place except I didn't close the bedroom door properly and Molly came in and jumped on my head. I told her to shush in case she woke anybody, but then I knew, just knew, I'd messed up again.

I got dressed and went downstairs and waited for Liz or whoever it was to turn up and take me to this 'unit'. It was no big deal, I'd just escape from there instead.

Only I'd have to meet everyone first.

4.

I never really did talk to Mandy and Marty, cos even though I knew I was leaving now and I might've been able to talk to them all right, I was shitting myself too much cos of this unit thing. Karen had said loads of times she hates those types of places, and she was as tough as old steak. It'd be like jail. There'd be loads of us all in one big dormitory, and we'd have to clean the floors every day and eat in a canteen with plastic tables. I didn't mind that so much, well I wasn't shitting myself about it, but I was about who else would be there. They'd probably all gang up on me and nick my smokes or make me give them my dinners.

Then I thought So what. I'd ignore them and if they tried to beat me up I'd thump them back—

I'd have to be strong to do it, that was the only thing. If I was feeling all weepy like with Kelly or sick like with Big Mamma Nurse I wouldn't have a chance.

5.

We were in the car going to the place. There was Liz in the back seat and some new social worker person who was driving. She was called Kate and I didn't like her either. Liz was trying to be all chirpy and getting me to talk and I wasn't, but at least she was trying. This Kate woman just drove, looking straight ahead with a face on her like someone'd choked her budgie. Even Liz thought she was a bit off I think. She said to her, all chirpy as well, —So, what can you tell Lisa about the unit then? and this Kate woman said, —There's six beds, and then she didn't seem to know what to say after that.

Six beds, that didn't sound too bad. That just meant five other people, so the dormitory would be small. And if there was three boys and three girls counting me, I'd only be sharing with two other people. But maybe it'd be all girls, and there'd be five people in my room. I hate sharing rooms, it was one of the things I didn't like about the flat. You want a bit of peace after being in front of people all day, you need your space.

—And the school you'll be going to is very nice, Liz was saying.

I thought, ??

Then I thought, I'd have to go to school I suppose, at least I knew they wouldn't let me not go. But I didn't want to go to a new one on my own. Then I remembered, and it felt funny cos it felt like years ago, but I remembered me and Nicola were expelled. We'd've had to go to a new school anyway. And just as well too, cos we'd have to keep out of Colabottlehead's way, we could take her no problem but her and a load of her Fake Bake cronies might be different. The thicker people are the less they seem to forget about things like bashing other people, so I'd bet my knickers that Colabottlehead was still after us.

But I hadn't thought I would be going to a new school, and living in a new place, on my own. I let on I was leaning out of the window so Liz and Kate wouldn't see me gurning. I was tired.

6.

We were here. It was somewhere near Portadown cos I recognised the shopping centre and the murals, but I didn't know exactly where. There was a big posh driveway and a big posh house. The car crunched over gravel as we drove up to the entrance. I'd been expecting some old grey building like the workhouses you see in films like Oliver Twist, but it was like a snobby boarding school or something.

Didn't mean I wanted to get out of the car, but. I sat there while Kate got out, then Liz with my carrier bags of stuff. They waited a second for me to move, then they both looked at me when I didn't. I thought again I needed to learn how to drive and how to hotwire cars, so then I could escape from things like this. But by the time I learnt I'd probably be sixteen then I could clear off anyway, they couldn't make me stay anywhere after I was sixteen. Just a year and a half to go.

I got out of the car cos I'd no choice not to. Going into the house seemed to take ages, I had jelly legs and it was like moving in slow motion. If it'd been a film there would've been scary horror music, and then the big wooden door would've slammed shut behind me like I near expected it to.

I was scared. It felt like a dream again, and I noticed stuff without knowing why I was noticing it. It was like I was taking photographs in my head. There was a lobby thing when we went in, with a table by the wall and a couple of bikes beside it. The floor was black and white tiles and clean enough to eat your dinner on. There was no way of getting past the lobby. There were two glass doors and a buzzer. Liz pressed the buzzer. I heard a noise, and she pushed the door, and we went in, and then it clicked shut behind us.

A fella was there to meet us. Small, glasses, short hair, geeky. He acted like we were his long lost cousins or something. —Kate! Liz! he ses, and then he looked at me and ses —Hi Lisa!, giving me this big toothy smile like he just thought I was the best person in the world. All these false smiles were really getting on my tits. I'd only been In Care for three days and they all did it.

I gave him a Look to stop his smile. But he just let on he hadn't seen it. He said —Come in, come in! and just as I was starting to think, Come in where? I copped on there was an office behind him. He started running about pulling chairs out for me and Liz and Kate. Then he sat on the table. Big smiles and sitting on tables, it must be what they learn them in social work school.

Liz started telling the fella about me being with Mandy and Marty over the weekend, and about getting caught in the hospital, and I sat there letting on I wasn't listening. Then she said —Well you know all the details, so I wondered what they were and what these people'd been saying about me. These people who didn't even know me.

Liz and the fella shut up then, I think they were waiting for the Kate woman to say something. She didn't catch on for ages, then she didn't even look scundered. She just said something about forwarding all the paperwork, and she'd be in touch to see how I was settling in. She looked at me when she said this, and she tried to do the Smile. I wished she hadn't, cos she scared the shite out of me. She didn't know how to smile, so I got a mouthful of teeth and a look like Freddy Kruger trying to chat someone up.

I smiled back, but just to stop her. Honest, I had to, she was freaking me out. But she got up then, thank god, and so did Liz and so did the fella. Her and Liz went out, and the fella came and sat back behind his desk. It must be time to get all serious.

—Right, Lisa—

They used your name in every sentence, too. All the time. There must be a rule book somewhere.

—There's just going to be an induction now, then you can settle in—

I didn't know what an induction was but it sounded sore.

In the end it was just your man going through all the rules and stuff, and it was so boring I stopped listening after about five minutes. I had to wake up every so often to sign a wee bit of paper, but then I just daydreamed again. I thought about getting back to the flat. I'd nick a bag or a purse on the way up, so we could have a party straight away. I'd buy the booze in the offy on the corner and just go straight up to the flat and do the code on the door. They probably thought me and Nicola had been lifted nicking something, so they wouldn't expect me at all. Maybe I should let on we had been, and I'd escaped…They'd ask where was Nicola, and I'd say – what would I say? Where was she now anyway, still in hospital? She was probably at home I thought, and everything was OK again cos she'd had the miscarriage. If it had of been a miscarriage. But I was pretty sure it was. Maybe she was upset about it. I couldn't see it but girls were meant to go a bit mental after losing babies so everyone said—

I caught on that there'd been a silence for a bit. I looked at the geeky fella. —Will we give you a wee tour? he said.

7.

Up the stairs there was the boys' cluster and the girls' cluster. A cluster was three rooms and a shower room and a living room and a bathroom and a toilet. There was a corridor in between them with blue doors that he said were the staff bedrooms. There was only me and another girl in our cluster the fella said, and there was three boys in their cluster.

The girl would probably be pissed off she didn't have the place to herself any more I thought.

You couldn't get into our side of the place, the girls' side, without a key. The boys' side was on the other end of the stairs and the fella said it was exactly the same as the girls'. Then he opened a door and said, This is your room—

I looked, standing behind the fella like the room would bite. Then he said, all bright, —Well, I'll leave you to settle in! so I went in. There was a single bed against the wall. Crappy light blue duvet on it that looked like it should be in a jail film. No curtains, just blinds. A wardrobe and a bedside table and a lamp and a sink. A poster of Justin Beiber on the wall that I took down as soon as he'd went away, I'd rather have bare walls than wake up looking at that every morning.

I wondered what the fellas were like in here. I hoped there was a nice looking one or at the very least that even if they were ugly that they didn't just look at me and think dog and not even talk to me. I wondered what the girl would be like too. Girls I meet all seem to be the Colabottlehead types, so I wasn't holding out much hope for this one. If she was like Nicola or Paddy or any of the rest of the normal ones I'd be OK—

I got bored with the room in a couple of minutes. I put my clothes away in the wardrobe and the chest of drawers and all my toiletry stuff beside the sink. And then I didn't know what to do. I wanted to go out and have a look round but I was scared I'd see someone. But after a bit I was dying for a pish, so I poked my head round the door then sneakied my way out into the corridor.

I tried a couple of doors then I found the bog. After I went I stood in the corridor for a bit cos I didn't know what to do. Then I remembered the living room so I found it and went in.

It wasn't that interesting. A couch, a TV and a table, that was it. I wasn't going to stay in there cos I was scared of someone coming in and catching me, but in the end I turned the TV on, really low, and closed the door and sat down on the couch.

I near died when I looked up and there was a fella coming into the room. I looked at him then I remembered what people always say about me looking all unfriendly and giving dirty looks, even when I don't mean to. So I tried to smile. But it came out all lopsided, like Kate's Freddy Kruger one earlier, and then I was so scundered I couldn't even say —Do you live here? like I should have.

—Do you fancy some lunch Lisa? the fella ses, and I thought Great, so everyone's been told about me and they'll all come up and gawp at me like I'm a goldfish in a bowl. —No, you're all right, I said.

—Are you sure? he ses, —there's just me and Aidan—

Then just as I twig he's talking in a posh accent he ses, —I'm Sean by the way, I work here as well—

I should've twigged earlier cos he looked about twenty, and I knew people were only kept here til they were sixteen. And anyway, I suppose this was the girls' cluster and living room, so if he'd got in he must have a key—

—Come on down, he ses, —it's only sandwiches but they're nice—

If there was no-one else about then I might as well. I went down the stairs after him. There was another living room downstairs, a massive one, with a pool table and the TV on with the lunchtime news. The geeky guy, Aidan, was sitting on one of the sofas with a big plate of sandwiches and a jug of orange.

—Help yourself Lisa—

I did. I grabbed a pile of sandwiches cos I suddenly didn't care what they thought of me. They'd probably expect me to have no manners anyway. I watched the news, Afghanistan again, I couldn't follow it. Then I went upstairs again and lay on my bed and smoked.

I heard people later, coming in. They were really noisy. There were shouts, and laughing, which scared me cos they all sounded like they knew each other and got on really well. But then there was a big row, I could hear a girl screaming and a fella shouting, then I heard someone in a posher voice shouting over them so it must've been Aidan or Sean trying to calm things down. It went all quiet after that. I lay on my bed with my heart hammering. I was shitting it, I didn't know why. I felt, I don't know, sort of like I'd broken in to this place and that any minute now someone was going to come in and catch me.

My door knocked. I near fell off the bed. I jumped up and ran over to the wardrobe and let on I was putting my clothes away. I don't know why I did that either. Surely it wouldn't be any big deal, me lying on the bed. But you probably weren't allowed to smoke. I'd sprayed loads of deodorant around but maybe you could still smell it.

The door opened.

—Aidan ses are coming down for your tea—

It was the girl. She looked older than me, but she was about the same size (fat). She had a face you could've sharpened knives on. I felt a bit better looking at her. I was fat and ugly as well but at least the only other girl in the place wasn't some skinny Tangoed blonde. And maybe she was a wee bit fatter than me the more I looked at her.

—Are coming down? she said, cos I was just standing there like a dick not knowing what to say.

—Aye, I said, cos I couldn't think of an excuse.

She came into the room a bit. She looked round in about a second but she seemed to have seen everything there. Then she saw my lighter lying on the floor and she said, dead quick, —Here, have you got a smoke?

I'd heard about this in jail films. When you just get in someone asks you for a smoke, and you have to say No cos otherwise they'll ask you for stuff all the time and make you do everything for them. It's like a test.

But I didn't know if I could just say No like that to someone I'd just met. She might think I was taking the piss and then she'd deck me. —Em, I said.

It didn't matter anyway. She saw my twenty deck under the bed and she just took one. Now I didn't know whether to say anything, or what to say. I didn't want her to think I was a wimp, but I didn't want her to think I was tight. Oh stuff it, she could have it, cos it saved me any hassle, and if she asked for another one I'd tell her no.

—C'mon, she ses, going out of the room, —it's ready—

This must be the big canteen bit. A big long table and Aidan and Sean sat at either side of it, and us, the inmates, eating off plastic slop trays with the food dumped into it with big ladles while we were standing queued up and everyone talked out of the sides of their mouths. We went downstairs. I was totally shitting it by now. I hate being shy. Nicola would've just bounced in and said Hiya to everyone, and they would've liked her, people always do. I skulked into a room behind the girl, trying to hide behind her. I could feel everyone looking at me. I wanted to cry.

I looked up after a bit cos it would look less dicky than gawping at the floor. We were in a dining room with two big tables. There was noise coming from another room beside it. The girl went straight over there, leaving me standing by the door. Did I go over? Did I stay where I was? Maybe it was something private and if I went over they'd tell me to piss off. But then if I was meant to follow the girl and didn't they'd think I was stupid—

I went over. It was a kitchen and there was a woman standing at a bench putting food out onto plates. The girl and three fellas were round her, all shouting. I thought they were shouting at her, but then I saw her laughing and heard them saying things like I don't want all them spuds, so she must be the cook and they must just be slagging her off.

They looked round and saw me then. It was weird the way they all did it at once, like someone'd flicked a switch saying Outsider Alert. I thought of Village of the Damned, but of course I'd've rather ate my own liver than said that.

There was a silence. They all looked at me. The three fellas were all typical fellas from round here, all spiky gelled hair and spots and squints and tracksuits. I'd already seen the girl. The cook looked like a ma.

The silence stretched. Even in my paranoid dome it lasted a bit longer than it should have. Then the cook smiled and went, —You must be Lisa?

—Em, yeah, I went, after another silence which made everyone think I didn't even know my own name.

—Do you want dinner, Lisa? (She used your name all the time as well), —It's pork chops and roast potatoes and carrots—

—Em, yeah—

Now I sounded like someone who couldn't talk.

—Gravy?

—Em, yeah—

I took a beamer cos I was such a dick. The woman held out a plate to me and I shuffled forward and took it. I wished everyone, specially the fellas, would stop staring at me. It wasn't cos they fancied me, I knew that.

I was the only one with dinner as well, and I didn't know what to do with it, where to go, did I wait for the rest of them or just go on ahead and sit down? I stood there for a few seconds that felt like a year. They all just stood there and looked back at me, giving me dirty looks. Really giving me dirty looks, not just me being paranoid. The cook woman had turned her back to dish more dinners out so she didn't see. I felt like crying.

Then I got annoyed, angry, raging, and I give them all a dirty look back. I didn't care if it was just me and four of them and they beat me up in the bogs after, they were ignorant gits. I dirtylooked them for a few more seconds, just so they got the point, then I turned round from them and went into the dining room.

So no-one talked to me. I ate my dinner at one of the tables on my own, just across from them all at the other table sniggering at me, and then I went back upstairs, and when Sean came up later to see if I wanted to watch a DVD I let on I wasn't well. He kept going, —What's wrong what's wrong, so in the end I said, —It's my *period*! to scunder him and he went away. I cried for a bit. No-one ever likes me and it's not fair. I'm not saying that like Oh everyone haaaates me, but it's true. People don't like me and I don't know why. I don't do anything to them.

I had a bath, ages later. I didn't know what time it was but I hadn't heard anyone come up the stairs yet so I knew I was safe. I used the bubblebath Mandy'd bought me, and I lay in posh smelly bubbles and felt like shit. Then I heard feet, loads of them, coming up the stairs. People laughed and banged doors and then they were outside the bathroom. All of them, the fellas as well. The door battered and I lay frozen in the hot water.

—Here, kick it in—

—Here, can you open it—

There was a big thud on the door, it sounded like all of them had ran at it at once. The door shook.

—Pick the lock! someone, the bitch, shouted. She was even more of a bitch cos she must've let the fellas in with her key.

The lock rattled.

—I've got it, I'm getting it—

I jumped out of the bath with half the water and grabbed my towel and threw it round me. It twisted and my tits were showing and I tried to fix it, to get it round me before they came in, before they all saw me—

They laughed again, outside the door. Then they were gone.

I lay in bed and smoked all the rest of my cigarettes and cried. This was rubbish, everyone here was horrible, they were going to kill me and I had to go to a new school as well. I had to get back to the flat or my life was over.

I tried the bedroom window, early that morning when everyone was in bed and the jail was quiet. There was a bolt on it and it only opened a wee bit. Fine. I'd get out, somehow, tomorrow.

8.

At least I didn't have to go to school the next day. And at least everyone else did. I lay on my bed and listened to the girl shouting next door and another girl, someone who worked here probably, being all nice and saying for her to get up or she'd be late. Then there was more noise, from everyone, then the door slammed and it was quiet. I lay on my bed for ages then I went downstairs cos I was starving.

There was no-one in the kitchen. But there was bread sitting out, and jam, and a toaster. I didn't want to make myself anything in case it wasn't allowed, but in the end I was so hungry I really quickly made two pieces of bread and jam, I didn't even bother with butter, and I ran up the stairs with them.

Someone knocked on my door ages later. I didn't answer. They knocked again, and shouted for me, but I just lay there.

—Lisa? Lisa, I'm going to come in, OK?

I got up pretty quick then. I was sitting on the bed letting on I was in the middle of something and had just sat down for a wee rest when the door opened. Some woman came in.

—Lisa, I'm Joanne, I'm your key worker—

What the hell's a key worker I thought, but I didn't really care. I just wanted her to go away.

She sat down beside me. She said,

—How're you settling in?

I didn't say anything. I didn't say anything the whole time she was there. Partly cos I think they're all the same, same as peelers really even though they let on they're not, but mostly cos I just couldn't be arsed. I just sat there and looked at the floor while she sat there looking at me and said she was there to make sure I had everything I needed, and to come to her if I wanted to talk about anything, and to ask the staff about anything, anything at all. She said as well she'd be 'lasing' with my ma and Paul to see if things could be improved. I near laughed at that one.

And she said she'd be getting me into the local school and I could start on Monday. Course I didn't tell her I wasn't going to be here.

She gave up in the end, there were too many pauses and her mouth must've hurt from smiling. But then she said I had to come down to the office in ten minutes for more induction. I was bored in my room on my own by now so I didn't mind but I let on I did. I tried to wait more than ten minutes to go down but I couldn't, Paul must've trained me too well and I was bored anyway. So I went down, and went into the office, and she wrote on all these bits of paper she called a 'support plan' and I had to sign all of them. I can't even remember what was on them now, something about going to school I think. All I cared about was nosying round me and seeing how I could escape.

I looked around the ground floor later. There was the office in the front, and the big room with the TV and pool table. There were other doors that were all locked, but they had labels on them like Support Room and Interview Room and Meeting Room. They were all painted blue as well. Behind them there was a laundry room with three washing machines and two tumble dryers.

Behind the laundry room – yes this was what I was looking – there was a door leading to Outside. I opened it and an alarm went off. Eek! I ran out the door thinking I could get away before they came out and killed me for the alarm. There were two big industrial bins lurking outside the door like a death trap, and I fell over one of them. I got up fast. The alarm was still wailing.

I looked around. Fence everywhere. There was a narrow alleyway and I ran down it, but all there was was more fence.

—Lisa?

And then there was Joanne, poking her head out the door.

I had to talk now. I had to let on I wasn't making a Bid for Freedom or else they'd be watching me all the time. I said,

—Sorry, I was just having a look round, and the alarm went off—

She didn't ask then how come I was standing down the bottom of the alley with bits of potato peel in my hair. I think she was just all delighted I'd said something. She said, —That's all right, and, —Why don't we watch a DVD? And I couldn't think of an excuse fast enough so I went into the living room with her and had lunch and watched some shite girly film I can't remember, the wail of the alarm still bouncing through my head. Denied.

I had to get away before the rest of them came back. And I had to do it with my coat as well, I'd near froze those couple of minutes out in the alleyway. But I didn't want any of Them to see me with my coat on, they'd cop I was trying to escape. So I was smart this time. I went back up to my room and I got my coat and the rest of my clothes and my shampoo and conditioner, and I put them all into one of the carrier bags I'd took from Mandy and Marty's house. I had to squash everything in but it was OK, I'd be putting the coat on in a bit. Then I opened my window the wee bit it could, and I pushed the bag through it.

Then I went downstairs.

I went to the office first, to see what they were doing. Aidan was reading the paper – like I say, great jobs these ones had. He didn't look up for ages even though I was standing there in the doorway.

—Where's Joanne? I said, when he finally dragged his eyes away from the paper and saw me.

He looked all delighted. He said she was in the next room phoning someone, but he could get her for me if I wanted. He must've thought I wanted to have a girlie talk with her about tampons and mascara. —No it's all right, I said, and legged it quick before Joanne came back and started giving me that sad doe-eyed look that meant I'm Listening —

Still, one down. And Aidan was a dimwit, he probably wouldn't notice if I sauntered past him in the nip. Still, the only other door apart from the alarmed one was the front door, and you could only get in and out of that by a buzzer Aidan had beside his desk. Like Fort bloody Knox, I tell you.

I had an idea then. I remembered the bath I'd had last night, and I went up the stairs to the bathroom. The window there opened all right, so without even thinking any more about it, I opened the window and dropped down to the ground.

I was excited now. This was great, I felt like I was in a film. I could hardly move at first my stomach was clenching so much. I dodged round the building, trying to see where my room window was so I could get my coat. But I could only get to three sides of the block, cos the fence cage beside the bins was in the way for the other side. I couldn't even see if that was the right side or not, I've never been any good at directions and stuff. And I had to hurry up, in case Joanne looked out of whatever room she was doing her phoning in, or Aidan finally stopped looking at Page 3 girls long enough to realise he had an inmate on the loose. So I just went.

It was easy enough, easier than I'd expected. I went round the side of the building again, and got onto the main path. From there it was straight down the driveway with my shoulders tensed up waiting for a shot, then onto the main road. I'd done it. I was freezing but I was free.

9.

I was hitchhiking. I was mad I knew cos of all the stories you heard about throats being slit and raped and killed hitchhiking girls being dumped in ditches, but I couldn't risk the bus cos I knew Aidan or Joanne wouldn't be long driving around looking for me. And I only had a few quid on me and I needed smokes. I'd be all right for food and drink once I got to the flat. I'd be all right for clothes as well, Karen always nicks stuff for her and Julie as well as stuff to sell, so I'd just borrow something til I got nicking something in my own size tomorrow—

I mourned my coat, but. It was about the only thing I cared about at that minute. I felt more pissed off about that than I did about right at this very minute being in some fella's car.

He seemed all right though. He was an old fella and he didn't look too pervy. He didn't even seem to want to talk so that was OK. I just gave him some spoof about being a student and having just been home to visit my ma and not wanting to worry her for the bus fare back, and he looked all pleased at such a nice display of consideration and manners from the younger generation. He didn't ask any more after that, and he didn't look like he was going to rape and murder me (I was prepared just in case, though, I didn't have my seatbelt on, so that if I needed to I could get out of the car quick. Karen had told me that). So I just sat back and enjoyed the warmth and thought about what I was going to do once I got back to the flat. I hoped everyone was drinking, and that they hadn't spent all the money they'd got today, cos I was dying for some chips.

—Where do you want dropped off, the old fella ses, and I ses, —Oh, anywhere'll do, so he dropped me off in the town. First thing I did was go and buy ten smokes, cos I was choking, and then I checked my money and I had enough for the bus up to where the flat was. I didn't even have to wait long for the bus, which was a complete miracle cos I was freezing, and by now I was in brilliant form. I'd go in and get cheered, and be given a bottle of cider or some vodka, and I'd have everyone listening while I told them about the Great Escape (I told my head to shut up when it remembered that Nicola wasn't with me this time so the fellas couldn't ignore me). And then tomorrow I'd go out with Karen and we'd go nicking, and life would start again.

10.

There was no-one there. I was a dozy bitch of course, cos it was only about four o'clock, so they'd still all be out nicking or buying the drink so no-one was answering my knock. But for god's sake, I was freezing, why couldn't just one person be in? I pushed at the door, just in case, knowing it wasn't going to work. But it did. So I went in.

All I was thinking about was the SuperSer, so that was all I seen at first. I ran over to it and switched it on, but nothing happened. It must've been empty. So I looked round the room for a blanket or a quilt, and then I saw that everyone had left.

There were still beer tins and drink bottles about, but I knew the place was empty. The cushions and blankets were away, but it was more the feel of the place, like echoey. Everyone was gone.

I went into all the other rooms and even into the bathroom, but I knew I wasn't going to find anyone. I think maybe I was looking for a note or something, but that was stupid I knew. I looked for me and Nicola's bags but they weren't there either. There was a pill packet which I thought at first might've been mine, but it was empty. Apart from that there were no signs anyone had even slept here.

I went back into the front room and sat on the floor and rubbed my arms less cold. I had to figure out what to do. I didn't think I could stay here, I'd freeze without the SuperSer or at least a blanket. I'd of lit a fire except there was nothing to light it with, so that was out. But if I left, and I didn't find anywhere, I'd have to sleep outside again and I didn't want to after the last time cos it'd been hell. And I'd no money for food to keep me warmed up—

I thought fast. The bus station, the airport, a McDonald's...where stayed open all night? The airport might, but I hadn't a clue how to get to it and I'd no money anyway. McDonald's would be open if not all night then at least til late, but I knew they wouldn't let me sit in there if I couldn't buy anything. The bus station was too obvious, bus staff were all gits and they'd move me on or maybe phone the peelers, and it probably wasn't open all night anyway.

So maybe I'd have to stay here. I'd just have to stay awake all night and walk about every so often so I didn't freeze. I near cried then, just the thought of the night ahead, and all the next days, no mates and no money and no food and setting myself up again. I felt like shit. I hated my ma and Paul.

But I still wasn't going to go back to the home.

Someone was coming up the ladder. I could hear them, the clink of shoes on the metal steps. I sat froze. It was the peelers, it was Joanne, it was someone who knew I was here, and I was dead.

I heard the door push open. Stupid bitch, I should've locked it! I'd been too rushy to see who was here to think about it. I sat froze still. They slammed the door loud like an authority. And then I saw the living room door open.

They saw me right away. —All right? they said.

It was Bonanz. I was never as glad to see someone in all my puff. He stood there smiling in the doorway, with his hood up and his hands stuffed inside the front of his fleece.

—Where've you been? he said.

I thought of where I'd been. Nicola bleeding, and the hospital, and trying not to get caught, and getting caught, and being in the sticks with Mandy Marty and Molly the mad cultists, and then being took into care proper, and running away…it was too much to explain. —It doesn't matter, I said.

—Where's Nicola?

—At home—

—How come?

I thought about that too. Nicola was at home cos her ma and da were all right and didn't bounce her off the walls most days. But I wasn't going to tell Bonanz that of course. I was still scundered about the whole thing and I didn't want him thinking I was a dick.

—She just wanted to, I said.

Bonanz didn't seem that bothered. I thought he was going to ask loads of questions but he didn't. When I saw Karen she'd want to know the whole story, but I'd've thought of a way to tell it by then.

I asked him where Karen was and where everyone was and what had happened at the squat.

—Dunno, he said.

—You must know, you lived here as well—

I could hardly see him cos of the dark and cos of his hood being up. —No, he said, —I just came back this morning and they were away—

I didn't believe him. But it didn't matter, at least he was someone, and I could find out later, and there were more important things to worry about. I said,

—Where're you staying?

He said, —Just round the corner—

I waited. He said,

—Have you got somewhere to crash apart from here? Do you wanna stay?

Thank god. Who said chivalry was dead.

11.

I didn't care about anything now I had somewhere to sleep. Bonanz might've been asking me back for his own reasons, but I let on I didn't know that, and I didn't care anyway. He could do whatever he wanted if I'd have somewhere warm to sleep.

It was a flat on the ground floor he had, and there was electricity. I didn't know how there was and I didn't care. There were two wee electric fires, the ones with the bars, and he'd left them on while he was out so the room was toasty. There was an old TV that was broke, and a kettle that wasn't. The room was tiny so it was really warm, and there was a big mattress with a pile of quilts on it. There was one of the blankets from the flat.

—So where is everyone? I said when my hands unfroze a wee bit.

—I told you, I don't know—

—But what happened?

I meant What happened, as in What happened when you went back the first time and no-one was there, but Bonanz took the huff. He said,

—I told you, I don't know, now will you stop going on about it!

I felt like decking him, but I'd nowhere to sleep so I didn't. I wanted to ask if he'd any money, or anything to eat, or some drink, but I didn't do that either. If I said Here have you any drink he might take the huff again and chuck me out.

I sat down on the mattress and wrapped the blanket round me.

—Don't get too comfy, Bonanz said, —you're going out to the offy—

He really was an ignorant bastard. He'd probably have me ironing his shirts if he'd had an iron (or shirts). But he'd said the magic word so I waited and hoped he was going to give me money for the drink and not send me out into the cold to do some nicking.

He gave me a fiver and some coins. —Get me a bottle of Bucky—

I didn't want Bucky, I didn't like it unless it was mixed with cider. But maybe the two bottles were for him, maybe he wasn't buying me drink. I wasn't going to say anything. I'd thought Bonanz was dead on but actually he seemed to be a bit of a dick. Maybe he was just annoyed that Nicola wasn't there.

When I came back from the offy he was skinning up. There didn't seem to be any food on the go. I told my stomach to shut up and I sat down on the mattress and gave Bonanz the offy bag with the Bucky in it.

—Here, he said, giving me one of the bottles like it was his first born son, —you can make a start on that—

I didn't care by now I didn't like Bucky. I was freezing from being outside, and if I wasn't going to eat at least I'd have a drink—

—Don't drink all of it, Bonanz said, —I want half of it left—

I couldn't believe I'd ever thought he was sound.

The amount of drink me and Nicola had bought him from our nicking! And he was shite at nicking, he hardly ever got anything. Me and Karen and Nicola were the best. It was us three who'd been buying most of the stuff when we'd been there. And Julie, but I didn't know how she got her money.

Stuff it, though. I necked a good bit of the Bucky in one and took the joint from him and shuffled closer to the fire. When he put his arm around me I let him. We sat like that for a bit and I wondered if he was going to make a move. I still fancied him a wee bit even though he was a bit of a dick, but I wasn't going to make a move on him cos he wouldn't fancy me. And it was him who was giving me somewhere to stay so it was up to him to decide if he wanted something out of it.

We sat and smoked and drank the Bucky, and all I could think about was how hungry I was. But then Bonanz was pushing me back on the mattress, kissing me and near sucking the face off me, and then he was on top of me. I had to pay him back for letting me stay so I let him do it. He was rough, and he did it to me again later, and again later after that.

It really hurt me, and I couldn't ask him to pull out at the end, in case he got annoyed. But I needed somewhere to stay so I let him.

12.

His mates turned up the next day. I'd never seen any of them before. When we woke up he went into the next room and I could hear him talking on his mobile. Then these three fellas turned up. I'd got dressed luckily as soon as I woke up cos I didn't want Bonanz to see me with nothing on, I was too fat. But I hadn't combed my hair and I knew I looked even worse than usual. I was scundered for these fellas to see me like this. I would've been scundered even to look in a mirror like this.

Bonanz hadn't said anything to me since we'd woke up. He sat on the edge of the mattress and smoked and looked at the electric fires. I was getting a bit freaked. Maybe he'd gone off me, maybe he'd thought I was crap, and he was going to ask me to leave. I wouldn't have minded too much right then, cos I was bloody starving (fat cow that I am). I wanted to leave and go nicking and get some food, but I was scared if I did Bonanz wouldn't let me back in later. But maybe if I got money and brought him some drink—

I was thinking about how to say to him about it when the three fellas turned up. They slouched in the way fellas did, and said, —All right, to Bonanz, and they just looked at me. They looked for ages, I started to get scundered. They didn't look in a nice way. They reminded me the way the OK fella had looked at me the first night I was in the squat, like he was trying to figure something out, to decide something.

The fellas sat down, on the edge of the mattress, near bouncing me off it. Bonanz didn't move either, so it was all getting a bit crowded. I definitely wanted to go and get some food. And I'd go on a big nicking spree today, and get loads of money, and stay in a hotel tonight if I had to. I look older than I am and I could make up some spoof for the owner. I'm a good liar.

—Have yis got the money, Bonanz ses.

I thought he was talking to me, that he wanted the money I owed him for the half bottle of Bucky I'd drunk last night, but all three of the fellas reached into their pockets, and they pulled out money and gave it to Bonanz.

—Lisa, head up to the offy, Bonanz ses to me.

I didn't know why these fellas were giving him money. I didn't know either if Bonanz would let me stay here and be his girlfriend and look after me if I was cheeky to him, but (just for a second) I didn't care. It was the same as in the jail films and in the home when the girl asked me for the cigarette – you had to let people know they couldn't boss you around just for the sake of it. So I said to him,

—Who am I, your personal slave?

The three fellas started laughing at that. I didn't think it was that funny, but I was happy enough to have fellas laughing at something I said, and I suppose it was funny enough. Bonanz was a bit miffed anyway.

—Go on, he said, —you can get yourself a bottle of cider—

Now he was talking. And by a 'bottle' he probably meant a litre, but I was going to let on I thought he meant a barrack buster.

He gave me two tenners and told me to get a bottle of vodka and twenty smokes.

—Do yis want anything, he ses to the fellas, and I thought he wasn't going to have much left if he was buying for them, I think he only had one tenner left. But the fellas all dug in their pockets again, and they all gave me seven quid each and they all said they wanted Bucky.

—And hurry it up! Bonanz ses, as I'm going out. Showing off. The dick.

I walked down to the offy and wondered why the fellas had given Bonanz money if it wasn't for a big carryout for all of us. Thirty quid they'd given him I think, that was enough for a quarter and a couple of Es. But I didn't understand why he didn't give them the stuff in front of me. I was no tout.

I came back with the drink. I hoped Bonanz wasn't going to go mad he'd no change. His smokes and vodka had been fifteen quid, then I'd bought a barrack buster for myself which was three fifty, then I couldn't help it and I'd had to buy myself a chip. He could have his 50p back if it helped, and I hoped he wouldn't throw me out.

My arms were killing me by the time I got back. I gave the drink out and sat down and waited for the spliff to be passed to me.

—What're doing getting yourself one of them? Bonanz started moaning as soon as I pulled my barrack buster out of the carrier bag.

—You said I could get a bottle of cider—

I was shitting myself saying it, and I could hear the yappy wee whine in my voice, and I hated myself for it. Why couldn't I just tell him to piss off, it was only a few quid and I'd gone to the offy in the first place and let him shag me last night so piss off you tight bastard?

—I meant a wee bottle and know it!

I wanted to shout at him but I was too scundered being shouted at in front of the fellas and if I opened my mouth I was going to gurn. —You can leave me half of that, Bonanz ses, and where's my change anyway?

I couldn't believe I'd ever thought this fella was sound. He must've had a personality transplant since.

I wondered again about what had happened at the flat.

I gave him the 50p, and he looked at it like it was the first 50p he'd ever seen, letting on to be all shocked. But he didn't say anything, thank god. He just sat down on the edge of the mattress. There was no room for me now so I sat on the floor.

—Lisa, Bonanz ses, pointing his vodka bottle at the fellas, —this is Janty, Davy and Gluebag—

A couple of weeks ago I'd've fell about laughing if I'd heard of anybody called Gluebag, but it didn't seem no big deal now. He looked like a wee gluebag as well, hood up and pale spotty face hiding under it.

He had the same wee weasly suspicious eyes as the other two. As most of the fellas I'd ever met—

Not Bonanz, though. I sneaked a look at him. He was all right looking really. I was sort of glad we'd done it, especially if it meant he was going to look after me. I wished I didn't feel so sore, but. Nicola must be right. It must be meant to be sore.

An hour later we were all a bit drunk, and Bonanz got up to put a different CD on. —Here wee girl! the Gluebag one shouts, come on over beside me—

He'd took his fleece off cos he said it was warm, and he'd opened his shirt the whole way as well. He had a wee weedy, baldy chest the colour of washing powder. He gave me the creeps a wee bit and I didn't want to go over and sit beside him but Bonanz gave me a look, and I didn't want to seem ignorant, so I went over and sat on the mattress beside this Gluebag one. He put his arm round me. I did what I did those times in a blue moon when a gross fella's made a move on me – I tensed up a wee bit and hoped he'd get the hint. It's not worth making a fuss, you just get laughed at and called a frigid bitch or a lesbian, and then ugly, and you end up being made a dick out of and feeling worse anyway.

But fellas should catch on, they must know rightly. How can they not? Here was this ugly freak throwing his arm round me, and I was sitting like I had a poker up my arse, as far away from him as I could get without actually throwing his arm off me. Why didn't Bonanz say something? If we were meant to be going out he shouldn't want another fella coming on to me. And we must be going out cos we'd done it three times.

I'm not stupid even though you might be thinking it. I know that doing it with a fella doesn't mean you're going out with him. I know fellas are always just after getting sex and let you think you're going out with them then they dump you afterwards. But we'd done it three times, and we'd liked each other before – at least, Bonanz had always been sound at the flat and I'd thought he liked me. He hadn't kicked me out this morning either and he'd bought me a bottle of cider, and let his friends see me. So we were different. We must be going out. But then why was he letting this fella drape himself all over me?

I looked at Bonanz. He'd come back from changing the CD, and he was sitting on the floor now where I'd sat, instead of telling me to move off the mattress. He wasn't looking at me even though I looked at him for ages, I wanted him to look at me so I could tell him with my eyes I wanted this fella's arm off me.

Then one of the other fellas said,

—What do you spend your money on then, Lisa?

Him and Bonanz and Gluebag and the other one all laughed like this was the funniest thing they'd heard since sliced bread. I knew I was having the piss taken out of me but I didn't know why. I wanted to cry again. Why couldn't people just be nice? Why couldn't they just leave me alone? I was always nice to people, I tried to get on with them, why were they always so horrible to me?

I couldn't let on, of course. I had to pretend I didn't know they were taking the piss. I had to put on a big bright smile and laugh and say to him, —What money? like it was the biggest joke I'd ever heard in my whole life, har de har.

They all laughed again. The fella said,

—The money get—

Then he said,

—For opening your legs to fellas—

and I was totally, absolutely, mortified. Scundered doesn't even come close. They knew I'd let some fellas in the squat shag me, and they thought I was a ***SLUT***.

I was so ashamed when he said that that I knew the only way to feel better would be to top myself. I knew it logically, I wasn't feeling sorry for myself. I was like, Yep, have to kill myself. Nothing had made me feel like this. Not even Kelly making me cry in the form room even came close, not even the day after I'd let the James guy shag me, not even getting caught in the hospital, not even Paul hitting me, nothing. The seconds stretched out, and I could hear my heart beating on my hot face, and I thought, Crying in school, big deal.

I had to say something.

—I don't, I said.

Shit. Shit shit shit. I'd've been better off keeping my mouth shut and doing what Hornball does of Not Even Dignifying That Nonsense With a Response. They jeered. That's another word the English teacher goes on about, and now I knew what she meant.

—Yeah you do, the other one, who was either Davy or Janty said.

The rest of them snickered. Suddenly I felt scared. I was in a flat with four fellas and they were all going to jeer at me like fellas did and my life would still be shit. They'd say next they didn't know how anyone'd ever pay to go out with me, cos they wouldn't even take it for free—

The one with his arm around me, Gluebag

Gluebag!!

leaned into me.

—Yeah you do, he said into my ear.

I think it was meant to sound sexy but it so didn't. My face was still hot cos I was still mortified but my blood felt cold at his voice.

I wanted to pull away from him and say again, —No I don't, but if I pissed him, them, off something made me know it would make it worse. Maybe they were just mucking about to see what I would say, maybe they would start joking with Bonanz or one of the other ones—

The fella stuck his tongue in my ear.

I pulled away fast, I didn't even think about it. The rest of them laughed at how fast I'd done it and at the face on Gluebag, all surprised. Slag him off slag him off, they were going to slag him off and forget about me—

He said,

—Ach now, c'mon!

and he leaned even more into me, and pinned his mouth over mine and kissed me so hard I was pushed back onto the mattress. I could hear the blood rushing in my ears, and the rest of them still laughing.

I didn't care now. I'd rather sleep on the streets than have to be snogged by this hoover just not to piss Bonanz off. —Get off me! I said. He didn't. I pushed him up and said —Get off me, would you !

He sat back a bit. I sat up, out of breath, and I looked round at the others. They were all looking at me, watchful, like cats. —Lisa, Bonanz ses, don't be such a bloody nun—

—What? I said.

—You heard me, don't be so bloody tight—

Are you expecting me to shag this fella in front of you all, just to keep you happy? I was about to say, but the fella lunged at me again and pushed me onto the mattress. My face was squashed into it and I could see the rest of the fellas watching me, not that bothered, like they were watching TV.

I felt a hand at the button of my jeans. I got scared then, more scared than I've ever been in my life, more scared than I've ever been with Paul. It hit me like I couldn't believe I was only copping on now, I was in a flat alone with four fellas, alone with four of them, and they'd been drinking, and so had I, and I couldn't go to the police if anything happened cos I'd run away, and who'd believe me anyway if I'd done it with Bonanz three times the night before —

The fella was trying to take my jeans down. I went mad. I might have let him later if Bonanz had wanted me to, but not here, not like this with everyone watching and the fella not even asking me. I kicked out hard with my legs, and pushed my arms out, and I managed to get sitting up.

I looked at them all. Something in my head made me know that if I let them see how scared I was I had no chance. So I looked at this dick Gluebag, and I spat at him,

—What do you think you're doing?

He didn't answer. He looked at Bonanz, and there was a silence.

Then Bonanz said,

—C'mon Lisa, you're getting a drink out of it as well—

The world had gone nuts. What was me having a bottle of cider to do with this fella jumping on me? Unless Bonanz was pissed off I'd got a big bottle instead of a wee one, and this was his way of freaking me out to punish me—

But I'd got the floor now, and I was going to keep it, even if it meant I had to talk even if I didn't know what I was saying.

—What're you talking about? I said to Bonanz.

One of the fellas, Janty I think, laughed. Just a short, hard Hah.

Bonanz looked stunned anyone could be so thick. He said,

—Will you get your knickers off, and let him do what he's paid for—

I can still hear him saying it. The blood rushed to my ears again and I felt like I was in a dream.

—What? I whispered.

The fella watched us both. Waiting for when he could move again.

Bonanz said,

—Are you thick Lisa, will you hurry up!

I wanted to scream, shout, stamp my feet, yell that I'd never been so insulted in all my life. But I couldn't speak. I sat there in a dream and all I could say was, —What?

Bonanz talked slow then, like he was talking to a child.

—Why do you think these fellas gave me that money?

—I don't know, I said, though I knew fine rightly now. I just didn't want to say it.

—Well you know now, Bonanz said, —they know what a slag you are and they want their turn—

All I heard was that he'd called me a slag, and I bit my lip not to cry, I near bit it through. Was I? Did everyone think I was?

Bonanz warmed up now that I wasn't saying anything.

—C'mon Lisa, they've already paid me, and I can't give them the money back—

I couldn't believe it. They'd paid him! And he thought I would do it, have sex with a fella, for money!

—I'm not a hoor! I shouted at him.

He was startled for a bit, but then he laughed.

—Course you are, he said. —What about all them fellas shagged in the squat? What about that fella Mackers told me about that you went out the back of the club with?

He was right. I was a ***SLUT.*** But still—

—They didn't pay me! I said.

He laughed again.

—No, he said, —they paid Mackers—

The world collapsed on me more. Again I whispered —What?

They were all loving this, enjoying the preview. Bonanz said,

—Mackers was pimping you, Lisa, every fella who shagged you in that squat had paid him first—

I knew it was true. I felt sick. Mortified earlier didn't even come close, and I thought I was going to puke.

But I had to save face. I don't even know why, I just had to. So I said,

—No they didn't! Karen would've told me—

—Aye right! he said. — You think Karen's your best mate or something, she was the one brought yis to the squat in the first place—

—She was just being nice—

—And she would've been just as nice if yis were fellas, wouldn't she have been?

Again I thought Yep, have to kill myself. I felt so stupid I wanted, really wanted to die. I'd thought those fellas liked me. I'd thought Karen was my mate.

Bonanz knew I couldn't say anything now, so he jumped in again.

—Face it wee girl, he said, —I'm the only fella's done you for free, and sure I only did it to break you in for these ones—

They watched me take it in. It was better than The X Factor for them, this. It's lucky none of them decided to make a move on me right then, cos I was so broken and sad they could've done whatever they liked and I couldn't have fought back.

But I wised up fast. I had to get out. I looked at the door, quickly, measuring the distance and how easy it would be to get to it before someone pulled me back. But it was locked I think, and if I jumped up and tried to get out they'd know how scared I was and then whatever happened would be worse—

I looked at the door and I thought Pleasepleaseplease let me get out of here, pleasepleaseplease. And as I looked at the door someone banged on it.

We all sat there froze, looking at each other. The bang came louder. We still froze, like this was going to make the person go away. Then I thought, maybe I should shout out, maybe I should scream Help, and see if whoever it was could do something.

But what could they do. And what if it was one of Bonanz's mates, and then by screaming out they'd know how scared I was? They'd make it worse, I knew it, just for badness.

Whoever it was hammered on the door now. Then someone shouted, and I've never been so glad to hear words in all my puff,

—Police!

It only happens in films I thought, but this time it happened to me. We were sat there like scared rabbits, and the peelers kicked the door in. I was scared and I gave them a dirty look, but at the same time I could've kissed them. I was saved.

13.

It was a drugs thing. Bonanz had a big pile of blow stashed inside the broken TV. I didn't see how much cos the peelers were doing their —Move along there now, there's nothing to see here, and pushing us all out into the hall while one of them had a nosy round. But I looked back at the door, and I saw a peeler lifting a big whack of blow out of the back of the TV.

I was shaking at how close it'd been when I'd been rescued. If it'd been a film I would've said Yeah right. But if them peelers had been ten minutes later—

I didn't get lifted. Well, I got brought down to the pigsty, we all did, but I didn't get charged with anything. I grassed myself up right away when they asked for my address, I didn't want them thinking I had anything to do with Bonanz in case they released us together or thought I had something to do with the stash of blow. It wouldn't have really mattered if they had I suppose, going to court doesn't mean anything to me now that I haven't got my ma and Paul ready to kill me for it, and I don't really care if the peelers think I have blow, but I wasn't going to share any of the blame for Bonanz. If it hadn't of been that I wasn't a tout, no-one ever touts, I would've landed Bonanz right in it.

So I only touted on myself. I gave them the name of the home, cos I thought at least it would be a bed for a couple of nights and then I could clear off again. So they took me back.

14.

They'd already phoned ahead, so the staff were waiting on us. I was scared a bit, in case they shouted at me, and I was annoyed at myself for even caring. Shouting at me was nothing, not compared to Paul. Or Bonanz and his mates – but I wasn't going to think about Bonanz.

We got buzzed in the front door, me and a fella peeler and a girl peeler. From the corridor I could see everyone in the common room, all gawking out at me through the glass door. I gave them all a dirty look. If they had of been friendlier I wouldn't have left in the first place. At least that's what I was going to say to the staff if they shouted at me.

But they didn't shout at all. They asked where I'd been, and was I OK, and did I need anything, and was I hungry. I acted all sad and pathetic, and they were really nice to me. This was great, Paul would've put my head through the door.

They got me some tea that was left over, and then I had a bath and changed my clothes. I lay down on my bed. But then I started thinking about Bonanz, and the fella pulling at my jeans, and I started shivering a bit. I couldn't get it out of my head, and I'd no TV or no music or internet to take my mind off it.

Stuff it. I didn't care what the rest of them did. I was going downstairs.

15.

They were OK this time. I should've copped on that they'd be the same as the ones at school and on our estate, knowing that if you were brought back by the peelers you were OK. There was no staff in the common room when I went in, and at first I thought I'm going to get killed, but then after they looked at me for a bit they started asking where I'd gone to, and why the peelers were there, and was I going to do it again?

They were fishing I know, and I wasn't going to be mates with any of them after finding that out about Karen, but I talked to them anyway. I didn't tell them about Bonanz's mates though, no bloody chance. I didn't even tell them about Bonanz. I just said there was a squat I'd been staying at before the peelers caught me, so I'd went back there, but the peelers had raided it.

—Did they find anything? the fat girl ses to me.

—Some blow, some Es, I said.

She looked impressed.

I said,

—We'd deal a wee bit if we were a bit short, you know?

I felt class. I've always wanted to be a gangster. I forgot about Bonanz and his stupid spotty mates. They're only spides anyway.

The fat girl was called Chrissie, and the fellas were Tommy and Petesy and Darren. We eyed each other up. I think they'd decided I might turn out to be OK, though they weren't giving me any leeway yet. But I hadn't decided about them yet either. Maybe they were being friendly to be friendly, but maybe they weren't. We used to do it in primary school, let on we were mates with someone, then say, —C'mon go behind the football pitch and play a game. Then you'd lamp them and they'd go back to the school trailing blood and snot and tears, and it was worth it even if you did get killed for it. I'd had it done on me as well, we all had at one stage, and I wasn't going to fall for it here.

Darren said did I want a game of pool. I'm rubbish at pool but I said aye anyway, and I won. I don't know how, I don't think he was trying to lose. But Petesy played me next and seven balled me in a couple of minutes and showed me up for the fluker I was.

Me and Chrissie played next. We took ages cos Chrissie was even more shite than me, but I won in the end cos she potted the black by mistake. Then Chrissie said she was bored and what'll we do now.

I didn't say anything in case she hadn't meant me as well. But I wasn't going to be mates with them, so I didn't care.

—C'mon go out! Chrissie ses, and that was me definitely out cos I'd no currency except the four smokes left from the ten deck I bought last night (I'd told Bonanz I didn't have any, and smoked his all night, no flies on this one).

But Darren said he was skint, and Tommy'd gone upstairs ages ago.

—C'mon go out anyway, Chrissie said, —see who's about—

Who was 'who' I thought, but I let on I wasn't listening. I didn't want to be mates with this lot, but I didn't want them picking on me either, so I didn't want to be scuppered by someone saying Here, what are you earywigging at biglugs. But then Chrissie said, —You're coming out Lisa aren't you? so I said —Yeah. I know she just wanted someone to go out with, but that was OK cos so did I.

16.

Petesy came out with us as well cos it turned out he had a fiver and he said he wanted to get blocked.

—Buy us something Petesy, Chrissie said to him.

He wasn't having any of it. He wouldn't even have enough for smokes after he bought his half of Bucky, so he'd have to choke all night.

—I've smokes, I said, cos maybe I'd be able to swap one for a mouthful or two of Bucky. Even Bucky was better than nothing.

Did we get pocket money in this home, I thought. They'd probably told me in that induction thing but I hadn't been listening through most of it. I suppose they must give us something, cos they'd be bound to know we'd go out and nick if they didn't. I couldn't ask Chrissie or Petesy though, I was new enough without sounding more like a tube.

Chrissie said,

—We should've thought earlier about going out, then we could've gone and lifted something—

—Is there nowhere open to lift something now, I said.

—Only the garage, and the fella who works there knows we're from the home, so he's up our holes every time we go in—

People in shops were

(had been)

the same with me and Nicola. We'd been stupid to try and nick that Man U top, the two of us. Karen was dead right even though she was a bitch, you shouldn't go in more than one at a time.

—Have you ever been caught in the garage, I ses to Chrissie.

—Are you joking, I've never been caught in my life—

—I got scooped once, I said.

So we started talking about nicking and all the best ways to do it and not get caught. It was probably my favourite subject at the minute, so I waffled away with Chrissie, and I forgot to be new, and to be scared I was going to have to meet new people.

Just as well, cos there was about twenty of them. It was like our maddest times at The Bridge Inn, a big crowd of people all standing drinking or shouting or snogging. Petesy got his Bucky on the way over and he let me and Chrissie have a few slugs of it each.

Chrissie was popular. Everyone knew her and the fellas didn't seem to mind when she hung off their arms and screeched in their ears. She had the loudest laugh I'd ever heard. The fellas gave her beer as well, and she shared it with me. I liked her a bit. She still wasn't my mate though, and I still hadn't forgot about her and the fellas trying to break into the bathroom on me. I supposed there was nothing I could do about it now.

We got two tins of beer each in the end, and some slugs of vodka, and the Bucky, and even a wee bit of cider. Someone had whiskey as well and they said it was stinking, so they gave me and Chrissie the rest of it. It was only half a wee bottle but it was really strong, and pretty soon I was pretty blocked.

Chrissie was blocked as well. I think she might've had a bit more to drink than me cos she'd nipped round the back of the block with one of the fellas who had the vodka. She came over and gave me a big hug.

—Are having a good night, she said, and I said, —Yeah, cos it was nice of her to ask, even though all these people reminded me I was missing our lot at The Bridge Inn and I was missing Nicola like mad. I felt really on my own. It was even worse now, after what Bonanz had told me cos I'd thought til then that even though I didn't have Nicola I'd still have Karen and the flat. But I was really on my own now. For the whole rest of my life I was on my own. And everyone in the squat had been laughing at me, cos Mackers had been pimping me and I didn't even know it.

I started to feel shite, like really shite, like jump off a bridge shite and not even being a drama queen about it, I mean really jump off a bridge. What was there for me now? I missed Nicola. I thought about us, drinking that Saturday night when it all went wrong, before we knew it was going to. Years ago, me and Nicola and Gonzo getting lifted, a whole different life. Gonzo! Who'd started everything by getting Nicola up the duff so we had to run away. Well, Kelly as well, cos we'd got into trouble for thumping her—

Where was she now, I thought. On the bed of some pond hopefully. But I didn't have time to wonder cos Chrissie started waffling away to me. She talked for ages, really fast, til I started to wonder had she maybe taken an E. She could've given me half if she had—

Anyway, she started telling me why she was in the home. She was the same as me, cos her ma had met a new fella who'd become her stepda too, and her stepda didn't like her any more than Paul liked me. She had a wee half sister called Stacey, but she was in a home as well.

—How come? I said. I didn't really care all that much, but I was being polite, cos I was sad.

—Cos of Him, Chrissie said, —the social worker was worried about her cos of what he did to me—

—What? I said. I wasn't really listening.

She looked at me as if I was thick. —What do you think? she ses. —Wandering hands, creeping into my bed at night when my ma was out working—

I was listening now. I'd heard about stuff like this, course I had, everyone has, but it's different hearing about it on Eastenders and hearing it from someone stood in front of you. I gaped. I didn't know what to say, so I just made a wee noise that was meant to sound like, That's terrible! and, I'm sorry to hear that. I couldn't believe she was just stood there telling me about it, with not a bother on her.

She said,

—Aye, my ma worked night shifts at Tesco's on Wednesdays and Saturdays and Sundays, and I used to have to stay in and babysit our Stacey. He'd go out, well not all the time on Sundays but always on Wednesdays and Saturdays. And I'd make sure to go to bed real early, before he came in, but he'd come up to my room when he did come in, and he'd get into the bed beside me—

What did he do, I wanted to ask. But I knew I couldn't. She said,

—One time he came home and he was really pissed and he fell asleep on top of me. I got out from under him and I had to sleep on the couch, cos I thought if my ma came in and caught us in the bed together she'd think I'd done it on purpose. So anyway, my ma comes in the next morning, and she goes, What're you sleeping on the couch for? And I don't say anything, but then she goes up the stairs and she sees him in my bed—

She stopped. —What happened, I said. I was trying not to sound impatient but I was dying to know, I don't know why. Chrissie said,

—She goes to him, she goes, Here, what are you doing in here? and he lets on he just got into the wrong bed by mistake cos he was blocked. But she knew rightly—

I didn't say anything, cos I didn't know what questions to ask without it sounding like I was being nosy, or a voyer or whatever it is. Chrissie was on a roll now, but.

—She goes to me, Could you not have woke him up? Like it was my fault he got into the bed with me! So I goes to her, No, how am I meant to do that with the size of him? and she goes, Don't you be cheeky madam, you could have woke him up somehow. Like it was my fault, you know? So anyway, then I just didn't care, cos she got on my tits, letting on it was my fault like that, so I ses to her, I ses, Aye, but he's not so blocked all the other times he gets into my bed is he—

—And she goes, What's that supposed to mean? and I ses, What do you think? and she smacks me round the face and goes, Don't you be starting with any of your lies—

She stopped, so I said, What?!

—Aye, Chrissie said, —lies, she ses! So it went on for a bit, and the bitch knew rightly what was happening and she didn't do nothing about it. But one day we were in school, and we were doing these debates in English, and it was about paedophiles and what should we do with them. And I wasn't on any of the teams, but someone on one of the teams said, Oh, we should help them and try and understand them, and I was like, Yeah right! They should all be locked up and have their balls cut off! So they made me see the school counsellor, and she said Why'd you say that? so I just told her.

I wish we'd have had a school counsellor in our school, I thought. Someone you could go and see who'd listen to you instead of saying That's nonsense, or Don't you talk back.

Chrissie stopped talking for a bit. We both drank our beer and drifted. I was thinking Chrissie's story was mad, and was there anyone in our school like that. There must be, law of averages. Then Chrissie said,

—So here, what about your stepda then? Same story?

—No! I said.

Yuk, the thought of it made me want to chunder. I couldn't believe she'd asked me, just like that.

She said,

—All right, keep your hair on. I was just asking—

If this was a film I'd probably have realised the Error Of My Ways here, that I didn't have it too bad compared to people like Chrissie. But it's not a film and I still think I had it pretty bad too.

It was a good night in the end even though I did miss Nicola. Chrissie asked me next how come I was in the home then, so I told her, and while I was doing that some people came up and listened. I was scundered at first talking in front of people like that, but I got warmed up the more I went on and they didn't seem to be laughing at me. They laughed at all the right bits instead, us getting caught nicking the Man U top and Kelly getting booted in the face.

I said about the flat as well but I didn't tell them about any of the fellas, cos even now even just thinking about that makes me feel like I want to die. But I told them pretty much everything else. It was cos of Chrissie, she just asks you stuff right out, really in your face, and you just answer without realising you're doing it, cos what else are you going to say, No comment?

Chrissie was asking me something. I came back.

—Are you up for it? she ses.

—Up for what?

—Getting in, she ses, —Petesy and Dee's away to get a car—

Joyriding, she must mean, did she mean joyriding?. But I didn't want to ask of course cos I didn't want to look stupid, everything was going well so far.

—Are you, Chrissie said.

I thought about the car crashing, for a sec. Then I thought about my ma and Paul, and Bonanz and his mates and Mackers pimping me. And anyway, I've always wanted to joyride. Kelly Colabottlehead and her Fake Bake cronies always go on about it on Mondays, they met so many fellas and got into so many cars—

—Aye, I said.

17.

It was me and Chrissie and Petesy and Dee in the car. Dee was this older fella Petesy knew, he was about seventeen. He was driving, he was good at it as well.

This was definitely a madder night now than all the ones at The Bridge Inn. But that was years ago and I was different now.

I was hyper at first, all adrenalined up, expecting the peelers or another car to come roaring round every corner at us. But we drove around for ages and nothing happened, so I started to chill out a wee bit. Dee was drinking though, a bottle of Bucky, so I was being a bit wimpy and shitting it a wee bit about him crashing the car. I wanted to put my seatbelt on but I didn't.

Then I forgot about the seatbelt, cos we were driving around Craigavon. It wasn't our estate, but I kept looking out the window anyway, just in case I saw any of them. I'd love to see Nicola. Maybe Dee would drive me round to her house, so I could see if I could wake her up by chucking stones at her window. But I didn't ask.

—Here Lisa, Chrissie ses, —you live round here don't you?

—Yeah, but I don't want to call in for a visit, I said.

Joking, I swear. But Chrissie got all excited. Thinking back on it I'm sure she was on E that night, she was too hyper. She ses,

—We should, but!

—What? I ses.

—We should call round to your house, give that stepda of yours a kicking—

And then pull the moon down after. I didn't say anything.

—We should, Chrissie said, —we should go round—

Dee heard us from under his Bucky in the front seat. He said,

—Where do youse want to go?

18.

We were outside my ma's house. We were outside my ma's house! It was the middle of the night and I was in a joyridden car and we were parked outside my ma's house. My stomach was pulsing so much I could hardly breathe.

Dee said —So what do youse want to do?

I couldn't talk. Chrissie said,

—Give him a kicking! C'mon give him a kicking!

She definitely wasn't all loved up even if she was on E, but then again maybe she just liked the idea of stepdas getting killed. She was bouncing round on the back seat, as hyper as a kid mainlining Smarties.

I wanted to give Paul a kicking. I really did. But we couldn't (could we?).

But I wasn't going to say anything. Maybe this was all some sort of test, maybe they were waiting to see if I was going to wimp out—

Dee rescued me. —Chrissie, he ses, don't talk shite, we can't just go in there and give the guy a hammering—

Thank god, I thought. They mustn't be testing me, so I didn't have to do anything. I turned round to Chrissie to back Dee up. She was opening the door of the car. I had ages to think Stop what are you doing – and to not say it. She was away.

She was running towards the house. We all stared at her for ages, her pale combats scissoring in the streetlight. Then Dee said —Jesus Christ, and he jumped out of the car and ran after her. I watched them in slow motion. It was like that scene at the end of Thelma and Louise where the cop, Harvey Keitel? is running after the car as they're driving it towards the cliff. I watched them.

But then I don't know what happened. Maybe the whiskey kicked in. Something did anyway, and my head shouted STUFF IT! and then there I was, out of the car and running towards Chrissie in my ma's garden.

We weren't fast enough. Or maybe our timing was great, cos by the time me and Dee'd got to the garden she'd picked up a big stone, from the rockery in the garden my ma loves ha ha, and she chucked it through our kitchen window.

It went mad after that. Petesy was out of the car now, and him and Dee were trying to get Chrissie away from the garden. But she was laughing like a maniac and screeching like a banshee, all —Bastaaaard! and —C'mon out here! and they couldn't hold her. She got away from them and was screaming —Bastard! bastard! while she picked up more rocks and fired them all through my ma's kitchen window.

I was shitting myself. But we were dead now anyway. So I picked up a rock, a rock from my ma's rockery, and I hefted it in my hand and I pitched it through my old bedroom window. The noise it made was the best thing I'd ever heard, it was beautiful.

Petesy and Dee were going mental now. They tried to catch us for a bit, but we were slippery geniuses and they couldn't. So they gave up and they just stood there watching us. We fired the rocks into the house, and we screamed as we did it, screamed and laughed and yelled, and lights were going on everywhere. Then the old bat at 508 opened her front door, and she shouted over —What is going on here? I shall phone the police! But Chrissie just shouted,

—Shut up you old bag, or we'll do yours next! and the old bag swung right back into her house again like she had elastic on the back of her nightie.

But other doors had opened now as well, and there were people behind them who weren't as chicken as the old bat, and they started to come over. I didn't care now, I didn't care about anything except seeing Paul. Where was he, where was my ma, even if they were out where were the two devil children and the babysitter?

I picked up another stone and went to haul it through the bathroom window, and someone grabbed my wrist. It's lucky they grabbed the wrist with the stone in it cos I was so fired up if they'd grabbed the other one they'd have probably got the stone in their face. I'm not just saying that, I was really buzzing by now.

It was Declan, the neighbour.

—What – on – earth – do – you – think – you're – doing! he gasped out.

I've noticed that about adults, when they're pissed off at you they talk like they've got a poker up their arse and a spud in their mouth. Anyway, when he said that I saw Chrissie looking at me, to see what I was going to do. So I wrenched my wrist away from Declan and told him to piss off and it was none of his business anyway.

And I threw the stone, and it sailed through the broken window of my old room and it hit the wall inside. Declan near fainted with the shock, me doing that right in front of him. He spluttered for a minute like someone'd pushed him into the pond. When he could talk again he ses, —It is my business, I am looking after this house – for your mother – while they're all away—

He sounded like he was going to have an asthma attack. But I was thinking Just my luck. I finally get the posse and the balls to go and kill Paul, and he's not there. Probably having a holiday to celebrate getting shot of me.

19.

We got lifted of course. The peelers were there even before me and Declan had finished the row, well I was kicking him in the shins by this stage and Dee was trying to pull me away. (I don't think whiskey suits me.)

So anyway, the peelers turned up and after that things went a bit hectic. It was all starting to feel like a dream again. We were in my ma's front garden and there were stones and rocks and bits of glass everywhere, and my hand was cut somehow and the blood was dripping down my wrist and onto my ma's garden path. It was quite a bad cut really, though I didn't feel it at the time. The blue lights from the peeler cars were on, and they were flashing on Chrissie's face and making her look like something from Doctor Who. All the neighbours were out now, and they were all round the peelers, all trying to shout their own version cos of course that was the most important one. The old bat from 508 was shouting the loudest, she'd come out the second the peelers got there. She was probably the one who'd rang them. She was still wearing her nightie, and a pink fluffy dressing gown, and all I could see was that she had really long, mingy, yellow toenails. She was shouting about the disgrace of it, and the noise, and she'd never been spoken to like that in her whole life, no she hadn't, and where were the police when things like this were happening?

I tried to act like I couldn't care less, but once the peelers did turn up it was pretty terrible. Obviously we couldn't chuck any more rocks, or kick the neighbours' shins, so we had to stand there while everyone gave us death looks and tutted and said things like, —If you were mine young lady. It was scary. I felt like a wimp for being scared, but I think I covered it up OK.

Chrissie just didn't care, no acting needed. She was doing these wee giggles, she'd look around her and then look back at the house and the broken windows and all the rocks, and it was like she'd just remember what we'd done and she'd laugh. Petesy and Dee didn't seem too bothered either. They were being all gentlemanly, standing between me and Chrissie and the peelers and not letting on they'd tried to stop us. They'd probably get into it for this just as much as we would—

The car! I thought of it so hard it near punched me in the chest. The car was sitting down the road a wee bit, and if the peelers saw it we were all dead. I really didn't care that much for myself, honest I didn't, but I didn't want Dee getting done for nicking it, he was nice.

One of the peelers came over to me.

—Right, young lady, he ses, —what's your name?

There was no point lying of course with a crowd of bloodthirsty neighbours round me, so I had to tell him. I remembered the night under the Bridge Inn another life ago, when we'd all given false names—

—And you live here? the peeler said.

—No—

508 screeched out right away. —Oh, she ses, —that's a lie, she lives here rightly!

—No I don't! I said. I was annoyed now cos what did she know.

—Yes you do, the old bat ses.

—I think I know where I live, thanks! I shouted at her. There was silence. A big tumbleweed went past. I thought, OK, not the way to get out of it here —

508 turned round to the peeler, mouth all pursed up disapprovingly like a cat's arse.

—She does live here, she said, like the school tout, —she's just away for a couple of weeks, that's all—

Ah, so that was the story. I'd 'gone away for a bit', like away to the seaside for the good of my health. Not out of my own accord cos of Paul beating the shit out of me.

(And Nicola being pregnant. But whatever.)

But I didn't get time to answer 508 back. The cop scared/startled the life out of me, cos he stepped right up to me and pushed me against the wall. Right in my face he shouted,

—That's what you are then, are you! A wee liar! You're a bloody wee liar!

OK, no matter how many times you hear about the peelers pushing people round and beating them up, it's still a big shock, and especially when it happens in front of other people. I was totally shocked. It was like with Kelly in the form room, knowing I was going to cry and rather dying than doing it. I couldn't look down either, or he'd know he'd upset me. So I took a big breath, and prayed that it wouldn't make me cry, and I shouted,

—I don't live here, right! I live at Apple Lodge!

He stopped then for a bit. You could near hear him thinking about it, the cogs in his stupid doughnut-filled peeler's brain creaking round.

I felt a hand on my shoulder. I jumped cos I thought it was one of the neighbours about to deck me. But it was Dee. He gave me a wee smile and put his arms around me and pulled me in towards him. I knew he was doing it cos he saw how upset I was, and it was nothing to do with fancying me or not fancying me, cos I knew he didn't fancy me but he was just being nice. And now I did think I was going to cry. And me and Chrissie had probably got him caught with the car as well—

It made me think later when I was in bed that it was the first time ever I think, apart from Nicola and even then, that anyone had done anything nice for me just for the sake of it and not cos it was their job or cos they wanted to get money out of me. He smelt nice too, and he was lovely and warm. I snuggled into his jacket and waited for the peeler to stop thinking.

20.

Joanne came out to the peeler station in the minibus to collect us. She was raging. You could tell she was trying not to shout at us, she probably wasn't allowed, but I could tell she was ripping by how white and tiny her lips were.

It was four o'clock in the morning, I couldn't believe it. Joanne had hair sticking up like a mad scientist, and no makeup, and eyes like pissholes in the snow, so I thought we'd got her up. But Chrissie said to me later they weren't allowed to go to bed if we were out, cos we were reported missing and they had to stay up and wait for the peelers to ring them if they found us. So no wonder she was raging. I felt a bit guilty. But then I didn't.

—Come on you three, now, she said, and when the peelers said there was some more forms to be signed I thought she was going to deck him. She signed the forms and then she near pushed the three of us out the door.

Dee wasn't being let go yet, cos of the car. One of the neighbours had spotted it and the peelers checked the registration on it and the bastard who owned it had already reported it missing. I really did feel guilty when I heard that. We'd all get done for it but Dee had only got caught cos of me and Chrissie. I felt bad for ages about that, I still do.

Chrissie was giggling again. She was trying to swallow them before Joanne caught her, but when we were in the minibus Joanne saw her laughing from the rearview mirror.

—It's not funny, Chrissie! she ses, which of course made Chrissie laugh all the more, —you were on a no-drink rule—

—Sorry, Chrissie ses, not even letting on that she meant it.

—And I thought you'd have more sense, Joanne ses to Petesy.

I waited for my turn.

—And you Lisa, she goes, —we're all very disappointed in you—

Why, I thought.

—You've let us all down—

And then she said it, Crap Line #62:

—And you've let yourself down as well—

She lost me after that. I'd have thought people who were meant to be trained to work with people our age would know better than to use crappy old lines like that.

Chrissie got me giggling too, and then Joanne did lose it. She was so pissed off she near drove off the road, but we couldn't help it and we couldn't stop. We laughed all the way home and we were still laughing as we got Up Those Stairs Now and Straight To Our Beds.

I couldn't get to sleep even though I was knackered. Too much had happened to me today. I'd woke up in Bonanz's house and now I was going to sleep back in the home, after a mad mad day. My brain was still buzzing. It was still only Tuesday night and I'd still been with Nicola on Friday.

I thought about Dee as well, course I did. About how nice it'd been to snuggle into him. About whether he liked me, or would ask me out. He was only about the ninetieth fella I'd ever thought stuff like this about. And they never did ask me out, so I knew I was kidding myself anyway. But I could have sex now, so maybe that would help me get out with people. I wouldn't shag Dee til I knew for sure he wasn't paying anyone to do it, though. He—

21.

Joanne woke me up about five minutes later and said it was quarter past eight. So what, I thought. I went back to sleep.

We were all standing in my ma's garden, only this time the front door opened and Paul came out.

At first I thought it was a monster but then the light from the copcar splashed on him and I saw it was him only bigger. He came over to me. He was shouting Lisa! Lisa! Lisa!

He was pushing at my shoulder and I was trying to get away from him.

—Lisa!

It was Joanne. For god's sake, could the bloody sadists not leave me in peace for a bit, it was the crack of dawn—

—Lisa, you have to get up, Kate's coming to see you at nine—

I didn't even know a Kate so I didn't have to get up and see one. Then it came through the fog that she was the one who'd drove me here with Liz, the one with the Freddy Kruger smile. I wanted to ask what she wanted me for, and why she had to come in the middle of the night, but I was too knackered. I went under the covers.

I could hear Joanne going to the door. Yay, I thought, she's going.

—Come on now Lisa, I heard from under the duvet. —I'll be back up at half eight so you can get a shower and get some breakfast before Kate gets here—

Bully for you, I thought. I went back to sleep.

They near had to drag me out of bed. A week ago, even a couple of days ago, I'd have got up no bother cos I'd have been scared they'd shout at me if I didn't. But I'd copped on by now, what could they do by shouting and what was the big deal when there was all the court stuff anyway. So I lay in bed. Joanne tried to get me up, then she went and got Aidan, but I went under the duvet again and wouldn't move, and I could tell they wouldn't want to pull the duvet off me cos they didn't know if I was wearing anything under it. Victory is mine.

Then they let the fire alarm off. Bastards. I tried to ignore it but it was one of them ones that gets in your head after a bit. So I went into the bathroom to try and escape it, cos when it stopped I'd jump back into bed fast before they got up the stairs.

The fire alarm was going off in the bathroom as well. No problem. Back to bed and two pillows would probably shut it out, and even if it didn't I wasn't getting up—

They'd locked my door. I stood there blinking in last night's clothes like Ozzy out of the Osbournes. I hadn't a clue what was going on in, cos I was so tired, and cos of this siren in my head.

Joanne came round the corner from where she must've been hiding to lock my door. She had a fluffy towel and some shower gel in her hand.

—You're up now, she ses, trying to sound all cheery. —So why don't you have your shower and Aidan can get started on your breakfast—

I was cold so I did. When I came out of the bathroom my door was still locked and Joanne was standing beside it with a change of clothes for me.

That's probably against my human rights, being made to be all naked and stuff in a public place. But I put the clothes on in the bathroom in the meantime cos I was still cold and cos I was hardly going to walk around in a fluffy towel. Then Aidan came up the stairs and into our wee cluster living room with some breakfast for me, and I was hungry and it smelt nice so I went in and ate it. And then Kate was at the door of the living room. Sneaky gits.

22.

I didn't say anything, though. I was cross cos they'd got me up. I told Chrissie about it all later and she said I was catching on quick.

Kate said I had to start my new school on Monday. She said I'd missed too much already and the sooner I got back to my normal routine the better it would be for me. I near asked if that meant they were going to taxi Paul in every weekend to lamp me, but like I say, I didn't want to talk to her.

Anyway, Chrissie said to just ignore them. They can't do nothing, she said. If you keep running away and nicking things and drinking they might stick you in a secure home like Guantanamo Bay outside Belfast, but that hardly ever happens, probably not even for nicking the car like the other night. Just keep quiet enough, she said, keep your head down and don't let them know what you're up to and let on you're not up to nothing—

I said that was an OK theory, but it was kind of wrecked once you started chucking rocks through windows at two in the morning.

—Yeah, she said, —you'll get caught the odd time. So you just have to make sure it's not too often. I hadn't been scooped doing anything in ages so they thought I was OK—

I thought of the other night after running away from the home, getting back to the squat and no-one was there. The worst thing was knowing I had to start all over again, on my own, start the way me and Nicola had when we met Karen in the bogs that morning after we'd left. It was like being at the bottom of a big mountain you don't want to climb but you have to, and it'd near made me cry. This was the same. Playing the game, keeping my head down, keeping my nose clean…years of it, stretched out in front of me til they'd let me go and let me be on my own.

I was sick of it all of a sudden. I said to Chrissie,

—I want to head off again, this place pisses me off—

—So do it, she said.

We were round the back of the building, hiding behind the big bin having a smoke. Same as me and Nicola a couple of weeks before, sharing a smoke and talking about running away. So much had happened me I didn't know where I was half the time.

Chrissie said,

—It's easy, I've done it a couple of times. Just wait a few weeks, save up your money and wait til they stop watching —

But then I thought of Bonanz, and the empty flat. I'd nowhere to go. Again it was like looking at a mountain you know you'll never be able to climb, and I felt very very tired.

I said, just to have something to say,

—So where'm I meant to go? I told you, my mates

some mates bloody lying bastards

have moved on, I've nowhere to stay—

—Can you not text them, Chrissie said, —have not got their numbers—

So far Chrissie hadn't caught on that I was probably the only person in the history of the world not to have a phone, and I wasn't about to let on. So I just said No.

—You'll be able to sleep out in a few months, she said, —it's getting warmer—

A few months was too long. I had to have somewhere to stay now, I couldn't wait til summer and anyway summer here was only for about a week so much good that would do me—

Chrissie said,

—What about money? Just nick stuff?

—Yeah, I said.

But I'd been thinking about that as well. It was risky, nicking purses and stuff out of shops. I'd get caught eventually. When I was with Karen I hadn't thought that, cos she was so good at it and so confident and it was kind of infectious. If I could manage it so I could stay out for a few weeks before getting caught then it'd be worth it, and they'd just bring me back and I'd just wait and then run again. But if I did that often enough they probably would stick me in a secure home, and then that'd be it til I was eighteen.

—I wouldn't nick stuff out of shops, Chrissie said. —It's too risky.

I wondered for a minute was she psychic. Then I said, —So what do you do then?

I thought she was going to make up some stuff about dealing, or doing some scams, like she was an Eastend gangsta or something. But then she said,

—I get fellas to give it to me.

I'd do that. No bother. I wouldn't have a month ago living in Craigavon, look at what'd happened to Nicola when everyone found out about her and Gonzo. But I'd already copped on that here it didn't matter so much, not at all even. And somewhere like the flat you'd be more talked about if you didn't do it.

And I'd already done it, and most of it I hadn't even liked and hadn't really wanted to, just the fella had said C'mon c'mon, so I had. So if I had to do it again to have a boyfriend and keep him and him give me money I would, no bother. It's just something you do. It doesn't mean anything.

I copped on that Chrissie was watching me, waiting to see what I was going to say.

—What, I said, —it's no big deal—

She was still looking at me. I got the feeling again that this was some kind of test.

—I mean fellas I don't know, she said.

Then I knew what she meant, that she got picked guys up and had sex with them and they paid her. I knew I had to let on I didn't care. And I even did let on for a second before I realised that I actually didn't care. At least Chrissie did it herself. At least she wasn't being pimped without her knowing it.

Suddenly the world opened up in front of me. It was like that punch in the chest again, only this time a good one. This was it, this was what I could do!

—Tell me how to do it, I said.

23.

She came into my room after we were all meant to be in bed, and she sat on the edge of my bed wrapped in her duvet and she told me. She'd done it with loads of fellas. The first time was cos she was with another girl, one who used to live at the home, a couple of years ago. Chrissie was twelve and this girl was fourteen. They'd run away one day, to Belfast like me and Nicola. (Maybe next time I was going to try for Dublin, like I had as a kid. Belfast must be the first place you look if you're a social worker.)

Anyway, they'd just run away on the spur of the moment and they had no money on them at all, not a bean. They'd got a lift up at two in the morning from some fella they were joyriding with. They were drunk and they just decided to go.

They got dropped off outside the city hall, and they were hungry and cold and they'd no money and no more drink. So the girl said to Chrissie, Wait here for a bit, and she went off. Chrissie said she waited on benches around the city hall for two hours, moving every so often in case a security guard or peeler saw her, getting hassled by drunk fellas and totally bricking herself the whole time. But then the girl came back, and she had near two hundred quid.

Chrissie said,

—I'd never seen that much money in one go. She told me how she done it, and I thought, Stuff that about nicking wee things from shops, and getting caught, and brought back all the time. I thought, That's how I'm making my money from now on. And her and me went out the next day and I got eighty quid—

I know I was only fourteen now, but Chrissie'd only been twelve then, and I was a bit shocked. Chrissie saw it in my face even though I tried to wipe it. But she didn't mind. She said, kind of bitter and soft and sad at the same time,

—Sure what did it matter. Hadn't my stepda already wrecked the whole thing for me anyway?

We talked on for ages. Chrissie must have knew I was thinking about doing it, cos why else would I have been so interested, but she didn't say anything like was I going to. She told me about the rest of it, going out the next day with the other girl, and them taking it in turns to get into fellas' cars. It's better taking it in turns, she said, so the other person can keep an eye out and try and remember what the fella looks like and the number plate of the car. Just in case something happens. Nothing had ever happened to Chrissie, but. She said it was easy money, and it was.

After she'd gone back to her room I lay in bed and thought about what she'd said. I was so excited I could hardly lie still. I wanted to go out and do it now. This was it, this was my passport. I thought that the only reason I'd been so scared in Bonanz's flat was cos he hadn't told me what was going on, and cos everyone was watching. If the tenners had of come to me instead of him (but I'd have bought him a carryout for setting it up), and if there'd been another room we could've gone into, then I think I would've.

So now I just had to do what Chrissie said, keep my head down for a couple of weeks, then go. Maybe she'd come with me. She wasn't Nicola but still, we'd be able to watch out for each other when we were getting into the cars—

You'll not do it, my brain said, you'll bottle out when the time comes—

But I didn't think I would. Seriously, I was sure I'd do it. A month ago I'd never have thought of it, but now I'd had sex, and I didn't like it anyway, so I might as well keep doing it and get paid for it.

It's mad, that fellas will pay for it. I thought that night it was mad and I still do now. All you have to do is lie there and let them do it to you, and they give you money for it. It's easy.

24.

But I didn't have time to think about it right away, cos next thing was, Nicola and her ma turned up. I was in the downstairs common room watching TV with Chrissie and Petesy, and Sean came in and said, —Lisa there's someone here to see you. Well they can piss off, I was about to say, cos I thought it was my ma, but what she was doing coming to see me I didn't know and she was meant to be away anyway.

Maybe it was Kate, I thought, so I went out cos I'd copped on by now it was easier to sit through their meetings and let on you were agreeing with them rather than having a big fight about it. All part of keeping my head down. But then I saw Nicola through the glass door. I couldn't believe it. I got up fast and got out there to where she was standing outside the office with her ma. She looked different. Glossier, shinier.

We screamed and hugged each other and jumped round in a circle with our arms round each other's necks. Nicola's ma and Sean stood there smiling at us. Then we stopped hugging and we looked at each other.

It was so weird seeing her! And here, in this place when I didn't even know she knew where I was. She looked really well. She was wearing new clothes, and she'd had her hair all cut and highlighted, and she was skinnier than before. That couldn't be cos of the miscarriage cos it hadn't even showed on her, but she did look skinnier. It suited her as well. Her ma looked well too, she always did. The two of them just looked like they belonged together.

I felt dirty and embarrassed all of a sudden, being stuck in this home while Nicola was standing here all shiny and happy with her ma. I don't know if Sean saw it, but he might've saw something on my face, cos he jumped forward and said in the bright social worker voice that he'd open the interview room for us.

So we trailed down the corridor after him and into the interview room. And we sat there and looked at each other. Then her ma copped on we maybe didn't need her, and she said she was going to see would they make her a cup of tea.

She went out. Me and Nicola looked at each other. Then we both said at the same time,

—So what happened?

And cos we said it together we started to laugh. We laughed the way we always did, for ages and til our stomachs hurt and I was wheezy and I thought if I didn't stop I was going to be sick.

It's only ever Nicola I laugh like that with. Chrissie's OK but we don't laugh like that.

Nicola got her smokes out and we lit up. The window only opened a wee stingy bit so us inmates couldn't climb out of them on the ground floor, so we knelt on the sofa and blew the smoke out the window. They probably wouldn't shout about it even if they did catch on, cos they would know that Nicola coming was a big deal.

Nicola said first. Just as well, cos now the laugh was wearing off I felt embarrassed again and anyway I wouldn't know where to start.

—Well the hospital phoned my ma and da, she said. —And they came up to get me, but the hospital wouldn't let me out for another couple of days—

—What did your ma say when she found out about the miscarriage? I said. This was the thing I really wanted to hear. Getting up the duff was such a big deal that when we heard gossip about some girl in year ten or eleven who was, we always said first, What did her ma say?

Then I had a thought. I said —It was a miscarriage, wasn't it?

I thought it must have been but it's not like I was a doctor.

—Well I'm not pregnant now, Nicola said. She tried to laugh but she didn't really make it. It was only cos I knew her so well I caught it, not just anyone would have. I wouldn't have with Chrissie.

I still didn't want to talk, so I waited.

She said,

—Lisa, I swear to god, I think leaving was the best thing we could've done. My ma and da were so glad to see me back and OK they didn't even hardly say anything about the, the, pregnancy thing, they just said I should've told them and I shouldn't have felt I had to run away, and that they hoped I'd learnt a lesson from it—

Bully for you, I thought. Shiny happy people.

She must've seen it in my face cos she said fast —And what happened you? Did you get lifted? What's it like in here?

—It's all right—

I was too tired to tell her. It was so much and I didn't know where to start and she wouldn't understand anyway.

But she knew she'd been what our form teacher used to call insensitive and tactless, cos she kept on. —But the hospital, she said, —what happened to you there—

I just couldn't be arsed going through it all. I felt like she would feel sorry for me, and if she did I would either deck her or cry. I said,

—The nurse got the social worker cos they knew we'd run away, and they took me to stay with someone for the weekend—

(I missed Molly)

—and then I came here.

Again she must've seen it in my face, cos she just went, —Right, and she didn't ask me to fill in any more.

And that was it. We didn't know what to say to each other. We did a bit of Do you remember? about the flat and taking the Es, but the flat was poisoned for me now cos of what Mackers had done, so I didn't want to talk about it. And I wasn't going to tell Nicola, cos she'd think I was a dick. (And she might think Sure god love her, desperate for someone to fancy her and kidding herself these fellas really did.) And we couldn't talk about before the squat cos that'd just make it more obvious Nicola's ma was cool and I was stuck here in this dump cos mine was a bitch—

She did say she was back at school, though. Reid took her back. That made me raging, cos I had to go to a new school. I was going to shout at Kate about that, it wasn't fair—

Anyway, she was at home and I was in a home, and we couldn't talk to each other. Maybe she was scundered cos I'd seen her having a miscarriage. Me and Nicola didn't even talk to each other about periods for god's sake, so me having seen something worse might have made her hate me.

Whatever. We couldn't talk anyway. It was mad, I couldn't take it in, that this was Nicola and this was me and here we were sitting like two oul women at a tea party. We did try, but after that first laugh and catch up everything came out sounding all polite. I think she was as glad as me when her ma came back and said maybe they'd need to be heading on soon but there was no rush. —Sure I'm ready now, Nicola said, and her ma I think was about to say something but didn't.

I saw them to the door, and her ma said about visiting again or maybe having me to stay overnight if that was allowed, and Nicola said she'd ring.

And I haven't seen her since.

25.

So that's it. So far, anyway. A beginning and a middle but no end. I'm doing what Chrissie said and I'm keeping my head down and my nose clean, til they're not watching me and til I have a bit of money. Then I'm away.

26.

I still feel shit most of the time though. Paul's not here so I don't get thumped, but otherwise I don't feel much better than when I lived at home. I've started school and it's OK cos Chrissie goes there too and she knows loads of people. And she said to me afterwards everyone said they knew from looking at me I'd thump them no bother, so I wouldn't have had any problems. I wasn't even thinking about thumping anyone. Joanne ses I can come across a bit aggressive. She's talking bull I think.

So I still feel like shite. But Chrissie showed me how to deal with that. It was after Nicola came to visit that time. I saw her out the door, and I was about to go back into the common room, and as soon as I opened the door to it I knew I was going to cry.

So I got upstairs quick before they saw me, and I sat on the edge of my bed with my fists against my eyes cos even if they didn't see me cry, red eyes were as much of a giveaway.

But it came. I couldn't help it. And once I started I was in floods, big hiccupping sobs that hurt my chest. It wasn't even cos of Nicola, that the visit had been shit or that I knew she wasn't going to phone me. It was that a bit, that I'd thought we'd be mates for ever and I knew that was it. But mostly I cried for the next few years. Because my ma had married a piece of shit, my choices were to stay in this home and get even more depressed, or run away and shag creepy old guys and maybe get killed by one of them. I cried cos Nicola was so lucky. I wasn't jealous of her, honest I wasn't, but it wasn't fair. She had a nice ma and da, and she was skinny and nice looking and everyone liked her. It wasn't fair. I hadn't done anything, and I had nothing. The next few years, no matter whether I did manage to run away and find another, good, place to stay, the next few years were going to be shite no matter what.

I still get that a lot. You know when everything seems so bad it wells up in front of you like a big wave and you know the only way to make it stop is to chuck yourself under a bus. I'm not kidding when I say that, or looking for sympathy. If I was looking that I'd say it to Joanne, and there's no way I would. Sometimes it near kills me to get out of bed. I wake up and I see my walls and my posters and my stuff, and I think, I'm me, it's another day and I'm me, and it makes me want to kill myself.

But anyway, as I said, Chrissie showed me how to deal with it a bit. Only a wee bit but it's better than nothing, til I decided for sure about the bus thing. She came in that time and caught me gurning. I was scundered but I was raging as well, you never get any peace in this bloody place. And she'd probably tell everyone.

She was only fishing as well. She was all, —Who was that? and —What did she say? and loads of other stuff. She wasn't being a mate at all. But I didn't want her to be anyway.

So she'd pushed up her sleeves a wee bit, cos my room was warm, and I looked at her arms cos I didn't want to look at her. They were the same as Karen's had been, all straight pink scars. I wasn't so stupid now though. I knew she'd done it herself instead of she'd fell through a window or whatever dicky thing I'd thought with Karen.

She was still going on. All, Was that your mate Nicola? How come she had her ma with her, she must be at home, and you're in here but yis both did the same things – and I just thought, Stuff you, bitch. So I said, —What happened to your arms?

She was pissed off. She tried to hide it but you would have had to be a blind idiot not to notice it. She got up fast and she flounced herself to the door. She said,

—I did it myself, you know fine bloody rightly I did—

Then she said,

—It makes you feel better. You'd be as well trying it yourself, get that face off you —

So I did. Do. I did it for the first time that day, after tea. I'd no razor, but there was a wee china saucer under my bed that I'd found in the cupboard and been using as an ashtray. I emptied it into the bin and then I threw it on the floor and broke it. I sat on the edge of the bed and started cutting my arms into neat lines.

It's weird, how it makes you feel better. You'd think it wouldn't, that it would just be sore, but it really calms you down. It's sore, but that doesn't matter, cos it's like it being sore on your arm moves it out of your head. And it makes you feel dead calm as well, just slicing, up and down, up and down, and watching the blood come up in a neat wee line and then smearing it over your arm. It makes you feel cool and tough as well, that you're hurting and bleeding and you can cope with it no bother.

It's only bad the next day, when it hurts where your sleeves are, and then a few days later when it starts itching. But it's not that bad, and it's worth it. I wish I'd knew about it years ago.

I didn't need to cut when I first Did It with a fella. Did it as in got money for it, not just did it. It was the next time Chrissie and me were out drinking. She said to me, —There's a fella looking to go with you. I was about to say —Aye all right, cos even though I don't really like it and it's just a thing you have to let fellas do, it's still kind of interesting in a way, and I wanted to find out if there's ever a time it's not sore. But luckily I didn't say anything right away, cos Chrissie said, —A tenner he ses, and I thought happy days, I can get some smokes to go with my carryout and maybe an E as well if there's any going—

She brought the fella up to me. It was scundering, but I don't think any more than it would be just meeting a fella the normal way (not that I'd know of course). —All right, I said, trying to let on I was all confident. —All right, he said. We just stood there for a bit, then he ses, —Do you want to go for a walk? and we found a field, and we did it, and then he gave me a tenner. It was easy, I didn't feel upset, and I didn't have to cut myself at all. Chrissie ses she had to once after, when she did it with some old fella. She said it was in Belfast, and she was on her own, and she wanted to hurry up cos everyone she was hanging round with then had already got their money and they were away to get a carryout to neck before going out. She was panicking she wouldn't get money in time and they'd go on without her, so when this smelly old fella asked her did she want to she said yeah. She said it near made her sick and that after she felt all shaky and like she was about to cry. When she caught up with the rest of them she took one of the empty beer bottles and let on she was going to the bog. She broke the bottle and cut herself with it and then she felt OK again.

I haven't done it for money again since, but I'm going to soon, and I'm not spending the money this time. It's getting warmer outside and the staff at the home think I've settled in well. I found a wee holdall in one of the store rooms and hid it under my bed, and I've already saved a few quid to do me for food til I meet my first fella. Chrissie might come with me but she doesn't know. She's met a proper fella and she's all soppy and in love and she ses she doesn't want to leave him. She's a dick, she's only been going with him about two weeks and anyway, what's the point of giving it away for free. He buys her drink, but.

If she doesn't come with me I'm going anyway.

It's Chrissie's birthday today. Any excuse for a party. We've gone into a field, way back from the road so no-one can see us from there, even with the big fire we've lit. We're all sitting round the fire.

I've got a big bottle of cider and a joint, and I'm sitting like a hippy looking into the flames watching the pictures. I'm thinking about Nicola, and the day she visited, and how I cried for ages cos I thought her life was better than mine, cos all I could see in mine was years of fighting and shagging and having to keep on my toes. But I was wrong, I see that now. What I have is freedom. Nicola can't do this, sit out at four in the morning smoking blow cos what are the staff going to do, kick us out? Paul can't get me any more either. I'm going to leave the home in a couple of days, and all I have to do is sometimes shag some sad old git for a bit of money, big deal. I'm totally free, and I'm on my own. Tasting the bright lights and all grown up.

Printed in Great Britain
by Amazon

66136922R00140